# CUPID GAMES

## RETURN TO CUPID, TEXAS BOOK 12

MCDANIEL, SYLVIA

**Copyright**

Copyright © 2023 Sylvia McDaniel

Published by Virtual Bookseller, LLC

**All Rights Reserved**

Cover Design: Dar Albert

Edited by Tina Winograd

Release date: February 2023

ebook ISBN 978-1-959689-04-1

Paperback ISBN 978-1-959689-05-8

Audio ISBN 978-1-959689-08-9

This book and parts thereof may not be reproduced in any form, stored in a retrieval system, or transmitted in any form by any means—electronic, mechanical, photocopying, or otherwise—without prior written permission of the author and publisher, except as provided by the United States of America copyright law. The only exception is by a reviewer who may quote short excerpts in a review.

Created with Vellum

**Games People Play**

Emily Martin, disgraced professional basketball player, is now the high school basketball coach in the small town of Cupid, Texas. Unfortunately, she's locked in a perpetual game of dodgeball with the boys' coach – her jilted college boyfriend who she's ready to knock out and send flying.

Zachary once loved the beautiful Emily until she chose basketball over him. And he's not about to help her succeed in Cupid. Not so long ago they were friends, but now they're enemies, and this time, he's going to spike the ball and leave her completely out of bounds.

Cupid has set his sights on these two and he's determined to have them meet face to face dancing around the infamous statue at midnight. But who will cross the centerline first and receive the dead ball penalty?

**Return to Cupid, Texas**

Cupid Stupid

Cupid Scores

Cupid's Dance

Cupid Help Me!

Cupid Cures

**Cupid's Heart

Cupid Santa

**Cupid Second Chance

Cupid Charmer

Cupid Crazy

Cupid's Bachelorette

Cupid Games

Return to Cupid Box Set Books 1-3

Cupid Help Me Box Set Books 4-6

**The Unlucky Bride

# CHAPTER 1

Instead of being a professional basketball player, Zachary Rowling was nothing more than a high school coach of the Cupid, Texas, team.

For the last five years, he'd worked really hard to improve his students – make the team better and win more games. Jayden wasn't a bad player, but Zach had spent the last hour showing the kid techniques that would improve his game.

It was late afternoon and they were working in the high school gym. Several times a week, he worked with players he thought showed promise of receiving a basketball scholarship.

These private one-on-one sessions were his way of paying back to those who helped him make it almost to the professionals. Almost. But not quite.

Jayden needed his help more than the others. In Jayden,

he saw himself and that was why he helped the boy more. He wanted to do what he could to make this kid successful.

Just like his coach had helped him get that much-needed college scholarship. The scholarship that took him out of Cupid and away from his family who self-destructed while he was gone. Now his mom was gone, his brother dead, and his father sat in prison.

"Block me as I try to reach the basket," he told the boy, dribbling the ball around him. "Put your body in between me and the goal. That's it. Your job is to stop me from reaching the basket. Try to take the ball from me," he told the kid, knowing he should have already tried several times.

The kid hit the ball with his fist, and it fell out of his hands and bounced on the court. Jayden pivoted, taking the ball and turning his back to his coach as he twisted toward the goal.

"Get low," Zach shouted. "Stand on the balls of your feet and shoot."

The kid shot the ball at the basket and it hit the rim and went in. The boy turned and grinned at him.

"Good job." He glanced at his watch noting it was getting late. "We've got five minutes left in practice and I want you to spend some time shooting the ball from each corner of the court and even from directly beneath the basket. The more you practice, the better you'll be. Five minutes of drills."

He stepped off the court and the kid began to practice what he'd been shown as Zach watched him. He enjoyed his job, but he would much rather have been playing professional ball. But that wasn't meant to be.

"Get low," he yelled. "Jump."

Standing there, he couldn't help but be reminded of himself at that age. The kid was the poorest on his team and needed a scholarship to go to college. He needed to get better or he'd stay here in Cupid with his drunken father.

And that Zach knew all too well.

At five o'clock, the kid turned to him. "I've got to go, Coach, or my dad will get mad."

He saw the fear in the boy's eyes.

"Good practice, Jayden. Tomorrow at the same time," he said.

"Yes, Coach," he said, running toward the ball racks.

The boy put the basketball next to the others and then hurried into the locker room. Soon, the outside door opened and closed.

Jayden's dad was a drunk just like Zach's father had been, and he knew the kid was working hard to improve. Sometimes kids needed a hand up to get out of a bad situation. Coach Roberts had helped him, and Zach would be forever in his debt.

With a sigh, Zach turned out the lights in the gymnasium. He went into the boys' locker room and closed and locked the doors before going to the teachers' lounge where all the coaches sat around talking.

They glanced up at him. For almost five years, he'd worked with these men, growing from a rookie right out of college to the head basketball coach. Sometimes he thought he would be here forever even though he applied regularly to different college programs.

He wanted to be a college coach and maybe eventually move to a professional team.

"Why in the world are you working so hard with that kid? He's not scholarship material," Kyle said, slouched in the chair, chewing on a wooden toothpick between his lips.

Kyle had gone to one of Texas's finest universities at the expense of his parents. Jayden didn't have that opportunity. Zach had not had that luxury, and Kyle often forgot about the underdogs of the world.

Maybe the kid wasn't scholarship material, but it was his only chance of going to college, and Zach would do everything he could to help him get out of poverty. In the years he'd been coaching, every season he tried to help at least one student if not more.

"He may not get a scholarship to a big school, but Wichita State, New Mexico State Aggies, or even Stephen F. Austin have programs he could be a player in. No, he's not Duke material, but he could still get into a smaller school and they would pay for his education."

"You're dreaming," Cody, the baseball coach said. "His father is going to want him to go to work with him in the construction business. The old man is a tyrant."

"He's a drunk. And that's why I'm helping him," Zach said, thinking the other coaches should be helping their kids in their sports.

It was a real possibility that Jayden's father wouldn't let him attend college, but he hoped for Jayden's sake, he could get the student out of here. The boy needed a break in life.

The other coaches shook their heads.

"Always a dreamer," Kyle said. "Well, fancy this. Guess who is going to be our new girls' basketball coach?"

The current girls' coach had to go on complete bed rest starting mid-January for the remainder of the school year. And while Cody had been subbing for her, baseball season would soon be starting and all his attention would go to that. The girls needed a woman coach to finish out the schedule, not a man.

Zach sank down in a chair across from the other three men. The coffee pot had been turned off and he figured they were just sitting here shooting the breeze before they left for the day. As the only single coach out of the four, he did his best to stay as far from the girls' locker room as he could.

"Who? Right now, our girls are in last place in the division. Who would want to take on a losing team and hold their hands and wipe their tears when they lose?"

"None other than professional ball player Emily Martin."

Oh, crap! His chest squeezed at the memory of the two of them together until the day he walked away. The way her lips felt, the feel of her body snug against his own. The memory of her sighs and whimpers when they made love. And then the knowledge that basketball was more important to her than him.

"Hey, didn't you two attend the same college? Duke?"

Oh, yes, not only had they attended the same college, they had dated until she'd stepped all over his ego and left him to play professional ball. When she made the announcement, there had not been any discussion on how they could stay together. It had been their last conversation.

"Yes," he said, knowing he'd never reveal their history to these men. "What brings her here? Who in their right mind would want our girls' team?"

"I think she needs a job," Max Vandenburg, the football coach said. "Last I heard, she was fired from the Washington Miners."

Oh, yes, Zach read all about how she'd had an affair with someone in the front office. Not something you did if you wanted to continue playing for the team. Upper management frowned on any associations between the front office and the players. Especially women players. Especially with married men.

"Yes, it's rumored she was having an affair with a married man in the organization," he told them, trying to contain the glee he felt. No, he shouldn't feel that way, but the woman didn't choose him, but rather her professional career. And look how that turned out.

In the small town of Cupid, being an adulteress would not go over well, and he could hardly wait to repay some of the pain she'd gifted him.

Why had she chosen Cupid? Did she know he was here? Well, she would certainly know soon enough, and he was going to enjoy tormenting her.

"Why in the world would a professional ball player come to a small-town school like ours? Especially one with a team who hasn't been out of the bottom of the division since the nineties," Cody asked, shaking his head. "Makes no sense."

The girls' team was hopeless.

"Maybe to hide from the world," Zach said. "When your name is spread through the press for the worst reasons, I would think you would want to crawl into the nearest cave."

The man must have been really good to spark Emily's interest.

"And our school board approved hiring her?" Max asked. "Hell, they did a thorough background check on me."

"Me as well," Cody said.

"Oh hell, guys," Kyle said with a laugh. "They want her for the prestige of having a big-name star in our midst. Kind of like the way they felt about Max. Sure, they checked her out, but they're hoping she'll bring the girls' team a state championship. You know how Texas's sports are. The home town loves for our kids to make it to the finals. And the superintendent's daughter is on the team."

They all nodded.

"Well, I certainly hope they enjoy bringing her scandal here," Zach said, knowing he was not going to make her life easy. There was a score to settle.

Max stood. "I kind of feel sorry for her. I loved playing for the Dallas Cowboys. The transition from professional player to coach is difficult. I'm glad I'm here, but damn, I would give anything to play one more professional game. Just one."

"That's different," Kyle said. "Who pays attention to women's professional sports? When was the last time you watched a professional women's basketball game?"

No one said anything.

"That's what I thought," he said. "Maybe the scandal made big news, but I doubt she even got paid a fourth of what the male professional basketball players receive. I doubt that most people even know who the Washington Miners are. She's a nobody and she's come to Cupid to hide."

It was true. Women's basketball did not have the same prestige as men's. Therefore the salaries were a lot different.

"Maybe so, but you know how a small town loves scandal. I just hope the school board knows what they're doing," Zach said, standing. It was time to go home.

Max headed toward the door. "See you guys in the morning."

Zach was right behind him as they walked through the door, down the steps, and into the employee parking lot. The cold January wind blew across the dusky concrete. Another five minutes and it would be dark.

"Didn't you date some professional woman's player?" he asked. "I could have sworn I read about it in the paper."

Zach cringed. He didn't want anyone to know about him and Emily. No one.

"Yes, years ago. But I've been out of college now five years. While I would have loved to have played professional, I never was good enough to make the team."

Oh God, how he'd tried. Training camps, practice squads, everything so he could make it into the big leagues. But it never happened. Always the same response. Not good enough.

Max nodded. "It's a tough life. I'm grateful for my time, but I would never encourage one of my kids to play professionally."

It had been Zach's dream. A dream he'd failed at. A dream Emily lived and screwed up. What a fool.

"See you tomorrow," Max said as he reached his Corvette.

The man still had some of the luxuries from his time as a player and Zach didn't begrudge him that. But luxuries were hard to afford on a coach's salary.

"See you," Zach said, climbing into his Ford F150.

So Emily Martin would be the new girls' basketball coach. Once they were lovers, now they were enemies. And he intended to make her life a living hell. Just like she'd made his.

Reaching into his pocket, he called his friend at the paper.

"Rebecca, how are you?"

"Good," she said. "Haven't heard from you in a while."

He laughed. The woman wanted to date him, but he wasn't interested. But he could give her a scoop.

"Hey, have you heard who the new girls' basketball coach is?"

"No," she said into the phone.

"Does the name Emily Martin ring any bells?" There was a moment of silence. "Look her up," he told her. "She was a professional basketball player who got fired for having an affair with one of the men in the front office."

A gasp filled the phone and then he heard her busily scratching information on a piece of paper.

"Why would the school board hire her?"

"Your guess is as good as mine. I know the superintendent's daughter is on the team and he really wants them to win state."

She made a raspberry sound.

"They've wanted that trophy for years. And parents are not going to be happy knowing their kids are being taught by a woman accused of adultery. We're still a small conservative town."

It was true. Though the town of Cupid had its own peculiarities.

"Nope, they're not," he said. "Anyway, I thought you might need to know."

"Thanks," she said. "Talk to you later."

He disconnected his phone and a twinge of guilt rippled through him. That was wrong, but still, retribution felt good. It seemed that Emily's professional career did not go the way she wanted.

And yet, he would never have believed she would've

gotten involved with a married man. What a stupid way to end a career.

People changed. And it had been five years since they graduated college, not speaking to one another. But soon there would be a reunion that he hoped he could somehow ruin for her.

Paybacks were a bitch.

# CHAPTER 2

As Emily Martin pulled into the teachers' parking lot, she sighed. The roar of her Porsche seemed to draw attention from other people parking their cars.

Not exactly how she had planned her life, but sometimes you took a detour on your way to excellence. And this was most definitely an alternate route to where she wanted to go.

Professional ball was so different from what she expected, but she'd been happy until Michael Devans sent her packing.

A shiver rippled through her. Paybacks were hell and she was gathering information on Mr. Devans that she hoped one day would send *him* packing. But until then, she felt fortunate to have found a small school in Texas that needed a coach.

From the glamorous life of a professional basketball player to a small town in central Texas, her life had taken a nose dive, but it wasn't her fault. And someday she hoped to show the world what a monster Mr. Devans was. For the time being, the Cupid, Texas, girls' team was in last place in their division and she would be fired if she didn't turn this team around.

The biggest question she had was about the kind of players she had to work with.

With a sigh, she parked the car and started toward the gym. The first day would be the hardest, and she just wanted to learn what she would be dealing with.

Waiting for her at the door to the gym was Mr. Sidler, the superintendent. Why was he here? The school was small and she could see they only had one gym.

"Miss Martin," he said, waving. "Welcome to Cupid High School. I'd like to talk to you for a moment."

Oh no, she wondered if he'd learned about her reported affair with a married man.

"Of course," she said. "Thank you for being here this morning."

"Let me show you to your office," he said, opening the door to the high school gym.

It was still early. School didn't start for another thirty minutes, but already, there were students practicing drills on the basketball court. Male students. Not a single female among them. That would have to change.

He walked ahead of her toward a group of offices with windows that looked out onto the gym. They were at the back between the locker rooms.

"This is your office," he said, walking in and closing the

door. A moment of panic filled her as the memory of being shut in with Devans had her heart racing.

Sinking onto a chair, he pointed for her to take a seat behind the desk. Relief filled her that he was sitting, but still she was aware of his every move.

Why did she have a bad feeling about this supposed welcome visit? But if they were going to fire her, wouldn't he have done it in the parking lot? Or called her?

"Our local newspaper learned about the reason you were fired from the Miners," he said. "I had hoped that we wouldn't have to deal with it here in Cupid, but we are. So I'm going to send them a statement. I'm asking you not to speak to the paper and hopefully this will die out in no time. But also realize that you cannot have any other marks against your morals or I will have parents screaming the place down."

She'd been thinking the news media would find something or someone else to spread across their front pages for the last two months, but the story just kept popping up. What no one knew was that there were other victims just like herself.

Adultery, her ass. In his dreams, maybe.

"No problem. I'm sick of trying to defend myself. People will believe what they want regardless of the truth."

Right now, she didn't want to alert him that at some point, the attorney she'd hired would be making a statement about the case they were filing in court. But that wasn't a topic of discussion for today.

"We're just glad you're here. And I can't wait for you to

turn this team around. Cupid needs to add the state championship trophy to its mantel."

He wasn't expecting a lot, was he? From last place to the state championship in one season. Sounded more like a miracle season than a realistic one.

She plastered a smile on her face. "We'll do our best, sir."

"Welcome to Cupid High School. Enjoy your first day. I know you're going to be busy. When is the next game?"

"Friday," she said, wondering how bad her players were. She had searched the internet for taped games and found nothing, which was unusual.

"All right, I better get going so you can get started turning our team around," he said, standing and walking to the door. "Good luck, Miss Martin."

With a sigh, she stood and bade him a good day. Her first PE class was in fewer than thirty minutes and the team practice would begin at three this afternoon.

As soon as he walked out the door, she saw the male coaches standing just outside her office.

"Gentlemen," the superintendent said.

"We're here to welcome our new coach," a tall dark-haired man said.

"Miss Martin, come out and meet the other coaches," her boss said. "This is Cody, the baseball coach, Brian the assistant football coach, Max Vandenburg, former Dallas Cowboy player who now handles our football team. And Zachary Rowling, the men's basketball coach."

Damn, damn, and double damn, she thought staring at

the man she'd dated and loved in college. The man who walked out of her life without so much as a good-bye once he learned she was going to play professional ball.

She shook each man's hand, and when she came to Zach, she gave him her best frozen eat-shit-and-die smile. "Zach, you're back in Cupid."

Not playing professional ball like he'd wanted.

Until this moment, she'd forgotten this was his hometown. And she'd never expected him to return here. After the childhood he'd told her about, she would have thought this would be the last place he would live.

"And now you're here as well," he said, his voice strained. "Did you leave the professional team behind?"

She didn't shake his hand since they already knew each other.

"Yes," she said, hoping he had not seen the articles claiming she'd had a marital affair. "I'm excited to work with the girls to improve the team."

The men all laughed.

"Good luck with that," Brian said.

"You're going to need better players," Cody said, laughing.

"Now, boys, let the lady do her job," Zach said.

The superintendent glanced between the two of them. "You both went to Duke. Did you know each other there?"

"Yes," Zach said. "Miss Martin was on the girls' team and I was on the boys' team. We won our division, but she got the professional contract."

There, it was out in the open. He hated her because she

got to play professional ball and he never was given the opportunity. Not her fault. Not her problem, any longer.

"Nice to meet you, gentlemen," she said, doing her best to be friendly, but not too friendly. "My first class is coming up and I would like to get my office set up and look at my schedule. Have a wonderful day."

With one last glance, which she hoped was not a glare, she looked at Zach. His auburn hair was still that gorgeous shade between red and brown, his emerald eyes flashed with a mischievousness she knew to be aware of. But more than anything, he still had that chip on his shoulder from when she was accepted into the professionals and he was passed up.

Get over it already.

Turning on her heel, she went into her office and closed the door. First meetings were over. Now it was time to turn her attention to her classes.

Glancing around the small closet, she knew the men's offices were probably larger, but right now, she was just happy to have a job, a steady paycheck, and not be dodging reporters.

Seven hours later, after the first practice with the team, she knew she was in trouble; this wasn't a team. It was a group of silly girls who were only interested in boys and the latest social media posts from their friends.

Already she'd had to ban phones from the court. When one of your players took out her phone and started texting during practice, there was a problem. With a sigh, she went into her office, plopped into her chair, and pulled out the notes she'd made while watching the girls practice.

Not a one of them would ever receive a scholarship in basketball.

She had her work cut out for her, and frankly, she would have liked to kick them all off the team and start over, but that wasn't possible.

In her office, she heard the male coaches in the teachers' lounge, laughing and talking, and knew she wasn't invited to the good ole boys club. But that was all right.

Time to go to the local gym in town and do her daily workout. Maybe she would never get the chance to audition for another professional team, but that didn't mean she wouldn't stop trying.

Picking up her purse, she walked out the door, ready to put the first disappointing day behind her. It was going to be a tough rest of the season that she could be fired from at any moment.

"Hey, wait up," she heard Zach's voice and sighed. She wasn't in the mood for him to come gloating. Or whatever he wanted.

He jogged up beside her. "How was your first day."

She put on her fake smile and grinned. "It was fabulous. The girls' team is the worst group of players I've ever had to deal with. And the coaches were so warm and welcoming and the superintendent came to warn me not to speak to the press. All in all, I'd say a pretty good first day."

Laughter came from him. "Not to mention a flame from your past showing up."

She raised her brows and gazed at him. "A flame? I'd consider it more of an ember from my past. One who abandoned me. Nah, he's the least of my worries."

"Still the same flippant smart ass, aren't you?"

Now that was funny.

"Why would you expect me to change? I like who I am. How about yourself? Has your ego recovered from a woman getting into the pros and not yourself?"

The man tensed and she could see he was trying to find the words to respond. Maybe she'd stepped over the line.

Suddenly a man ran toward them.

"Miss Martin, can we have a word with you?"

"He's a reporter," Zach warned.

"Gotta go," she said. "If I'd gotten this kind of press while I was playing, it wouldn't have mattered what that jerk accused me of."

"Accused you of? I find that hard to believe. You must have been desperate to sleep with a married man."

It was all she could do not to turn and throw a punch at him. But fighting in the teachers' parking lot on her first day in front of a reporter would probably get her canned really quick.

Ignoring his comment, she jogged to her car, climbed in, and started the Porsche. Her one extravagant purchase for herself while she was playing. After all, the star player deserved to be a little arrogant.

"Hey," Zach said, running up to the car. "My boys get the court from three to five tomorrow."

Rolling the window down, she shook her head.

"No," she said. "My girls get the court from three to five every other day. Maybe that's why Cupid has the worst girls' team in the division. The boys not sharing."

"You had the court today and I'll have it tomorrow," she said, looking at his scowling face. "I've already told the girls to be there."

"And I told my boys to be there," he said.

"Too bad, deal with it," she said and backed the Porsche out of the parking place.

Already she could tell he was going to do everything he could to make her life miserable.

But the worst thing was that time had only made him more handsome. Shame he couldn't deal with her being accepted into pro ball and not him.

# CHAPTER 3

The next day, Zach took his boys to the outside court. No, it wasn't as nice as the inside court, but he wanted to lure her into believing she had won. Oh no, the battle royale had not even begun yet.

And he didn't know what to think about her disagreeing about the adultery. The papers said she had an affair with a married man. He'd not known how to respond, and if it was true, he was not wrong to contact the paper.

And yet why would the man turn her in if he was married? Wouldn't he be trying to hide this affair from his wife? Something felt off, but Zach was going to take advantage of the situation.

This was revenge.

Though somehow it didn't feel as good as he'd hoped. In fact, he was regretting what he'd done already.

Watching his boys practice, his mind drifted in and out of the past. The kids were playing well today, though being outside, their attention was often distracted when a teenage girl walked by or one of their buddies called to them.

At the end of his practice with his team, he told them to hit the showers. Tomorrow, they would have the inside court.

The kids ran into the building excitedly. One week to their next game, and tomorrow he would strategize with them. They were going to beat the Granbury team just to show up the girls. They had not won a game all season.

When he walked into the gym, Emily had her girls sitting on the floor as she walked around them, talking.

"I was hired by the superintendent to turn a losing team into winners. That's what I plan to do. Each of you needs to decide if you want to be on a winning basketball team or if playing ball is not important to you. If you want to quit, I'll help you get your schedule changed, so you can go do something you love. It's your choice.

"But if you decide to stay, there are going to be tryouts. No one is guaranteed a position. No one. For two days, I've watched you girls and some of you are in the wrong place. Some of you don't give two flips about basketball, and some of you are just hanging with your friends. I want dedicated players. I want a cohesive team. I want girls who crave the championship."

Now that was funny. These girls couldn't care less about basketball.

She stopped in front of them. "New rule. On the days we're practicing outside, like tomorrow, we meet at six a.m. to practice before school."

There was a round of groans.

"Do you want to play basketball? Do you want a winning team? Your choice. Six a.m. in the morning. Don't be late unless you want to do laps. Now, hit the showers."

The girls slowly stood and walked to the locker room. Some of them were grumbling about how they missed their old coach.

"Six a.m. practice?" he said, walking over to her. "They're going to hate you."

This could work to his advantage. The superintendent's daughter played on the team and she was always trouble. She would rally these girls against Emily and she'd soon be gone.

"You got a problem with that? I would think you would love for my girls to hate me. Are your boys going to be practicing at that time?"

"Oh no," he said. "The gym is yours. I'm sure their parents are going to love dropping them off that early in the morning."

She shrugged. "Good, I plan on putting the gym to good use. As for their parents, they'll thank me when we have a winning team," she said and started to walk away, then she turned to him.

"A little birdie told me that you contacted the papers. Did you tell them about my scandal?"

He'd never been good at lying, and he didn't want to

start now. Maybe it would be good to show her that he was not on her side.

"Yes, I did," he said, grinning. "I thought the parents of Cupid, Texas, needed to know who their daughters' new coach was and how she'd been run out of professional ball."

She walked over to him and smiled.

"Keep going, Zach. Keep making my life even more miserable, and I'll repay the favor. I could always tell them how when you learned I was going into professional basketball, you dropped me faster than lightning. Which could only mean that you were so damn jealous, you couldn't stand it."

She poked her finger in his chest and he took a step back.

Damn, but she was right. At the time, he'd not realized that part of his problem was she'd been accepted and not one team tried to get his attention. At the time, he believed she chose basketball over him. And she had.

"At least I didn't choose basketball over you," he said, his voice low.

She started laughing. "The hell you didn't. You would have given your right nut to play professional ball. I would have been dust in the wind and you would have been on the next plane out of town. Don't lie to yourself, Rowling. It isn't becoming. Makes you look weak."

With that, she turned and walked away. Over her shoulder, she said, "See you tomorrow. Have a great night and be sure to drive through town."

Drive through town? What was she talking about? Why would he drive through town?

With a sigh, he headed to his office, her words disturbing him. Had he really been jealous? Of course, he had. She was right. He would have sacrificed his right nut and even his left one to play professional basketball. But it wasn't meant to happen.

Brian met him at the door to his office, a grin on his face as he stood with his arms crossed like he knew what was going on.

"You hitting on the new coach," Brian asked.

Hell, he'd hit on her nearly six years ago, gotten into her bed, and even planned on asking her to marry him until she left him reeling.

"Absolutely not," he said. He was tempted to say *been there, done that, and have the scarred heart to go with it,* but he kept his thoughts bundled inside his head. No need for the biggest gossip in school to learn they dated in college.

"Did you read that article in the paper this morning?"

"No, I haven't had time yet," Zach said, regretting turning the paper on to her story. He'd let his thirst for revenge get ahead of his logic. Now there were reporters on school grounds. And she knew he'd been the one to contact them.

"If we don't have upset parents marching down here, I'll be shocked. Why they hired her is beyond me," the man said. "Though she sure has made the scenery around here a lot better. Auburn hair and sparkling blue eyes and curves that make a man think of how those well-rounded shapes would feel in his hands."

Zach did not like where this conversation was going at all. In fact, it disturbed him. "You're married."

"A man can still look and dream," he said then laughed.

If Brian got even a hint that his words were upsetting him, Zach knew the man would make his life absolute hell. More hellish than it was right now. Because Emily looked good. Absolutely freaking delicious like a platter he wanted to taste whatever she offered. A platter where the food would be so yummy, he'd want seconds and thirds.

"What are you guys talking about?" Cody said, walking up beside them.

"We're talking about our new coach and how she doesn't stand a chance in hell of lasting here," Brian said, grinning. "But she's sure nice to look at while she's here."

Cody shook his head. "You're treading on dangerous ground, my friend. All you need is to get called to the superintendent's office for sexual harassment."

"I'm not harassing her. I'm just looking," Brian said. "Can't a man gaze at a beautiful woman?"

"Not in today's world," Zach replied, wanting the man to stop. Wishing he would just shut up.

"Tell that to your wife," Cody warned. "See what she thinks of your description of our newest coach."

Zach had had enough. It was hard enough having to work beside Emily without hearing this. And he couldn't tell the man to shut up or face interrogation.

The best thing to do was leave.

"Good night, guys," he said as he turned to the door. It was time to get out of here or he feared his facial expression would be the tell that Brian would pounce on.

"Watch out for the reporters outside," Cody yelled.

Great, just great.

As he walked outside, he saw the waiting group of eager magpies. They had grown from just the local press to the Dallas area and even a few national reporters that he recognized.

She was a hot commodity in the news department. That one phone call had now created a major shitstorm all because of him.

"Mr. Rowling, tell us your feelings about the new coach," one screamed.

What could he say? Gazing at her, he knew he wanted to jump back in her bed, but that would never happen. If he had his way, he would slowly peel her shorts and top from those long slim legs and explore every inch of her well-endowed body.

"I'm happy for the girls' team. I hope she can turn these girls into athletes," he said and wanted to add *rather than just teenage party girls,* which was what they were. The woman was up against a monumental task. She shouldn't sign more than a six-month contract because she wouldn't be here long.

Her future looked dim.

He walked down the stairs exiting the gym.

"What about the sign on your car," someone yelled. "What do you think about that?"

"What are you talking about?"

"Look at the back of your truck. Some kid is punking you," the man said with a laugh.

Hurrying into the parking lot, he went to his truck. Hanging on the back of his Ford F-150 was a hand-painted sign.

*Professional Basketball Reject!*

Like a volcano, the rage exploded through him. Taking a deep breath to calm his anger, he tried to yank the sign off his truck, but it was tied on securely. With hands shaking, he had to patiently untwist the wires holding the sign on his tailgate.

That bitch! This wasn't some random high school student; this was Emily.

And yet part of him reminded him that he was the one who started this war. He contacted the newspaper. This was payback.

"Thanks," he said, waving to the newspaper reporter.

And what had she said earlier to him? Be sure to ride through town. Thank goodness, the reporter had told him in advance.

Carrying the sign, he went back inside the gym. Going to her office, he took the sign and tied it to her office door. Then he went into the girls' locker room and removed all the towels. In the morning after her girls worked out, they would not have any towels to dry off with.

Score two for him.

With a snicker, he left the gym and went to his truck.

She had just declared war and he was ready to reciprocate.

Game on!

# CHAPTER 4

Emily walked in and threw her purse on the couch, glanced around the small apartment, and sighed. What in the hell was she doing?

She was playing a dangerous game with Zach, and she feared where it would soon end. Because of her background, she knew they would not hesitate to rid themselves of a lecherous woman who went after her professional team staff members.

But it wasn't true, and she was so tired of fighting this battle and always coming out the loser.

Reaching over to the phone message machine, she pushed the flashing button. Yes, she still had the old-timey recorder, because after the scandal, her life had been hell. She never answered the phone and let the machine do all the talking. That way, she could save herself the embarrassment, especially after the jerk had given her number to the press.

And, of course, someone leaked it to a group who thought they should call and harass her and tell her what a terrible person she was to break up a family.

Innocent until proven guilty was a thing of the past. Now it seemed she was guilty until someone proved him wrong. She'd done nothing wrong.

Nothing, except fend off his unwanted advances. Tell him there was nothing that would ever coerce her into his bed. So he retaliated.

Professional basketball had been her dream, but it cost her a very important relationship with Zach, and now this jerk in the front office who thought he could force her into his bed.

Didn't work.

Never would.

But in the meantime, she'd lost her dream career. And no other team in basketball would touch her now. From star player to radioactive loser.

With a sigh, she hit the button and listened to several robo-calls before she heard the call she was looking for.

"Call me. I know you're trying to lay low, but I've found another girl. We now have three and I think there are probably several more. We need to talk."

It was late, but she couldn't wait. Besides, tomorrow, her day would start at four a.m. She would be at the school before it opened to welcome the girls who cared about the team. This was their first real test and the ones who didn't show...well, they would soon find themselves searching for a new class at the same time.

Her so-called "star" player thought nothing could get her in trouble, but she was wrong and Emily had the strangest feeling she was going to test her.

But, first, she had to make this phone call and then she wanted to go over some new drills they were learning tomorrow morning.

Quickly she dialed her lawyer's number.

He picked up almost immediately. "I thought I'd be hearing from you as soon as you heard my message."

"Good job, Allen. I'm so pleased," she said. "How many more do we need to find?"

"I'd like two more. If there are five women, there are possibly even more and we could have additional ones come forward once we announce our lawsuit. But once we have five, I'll draw up the paperwork and we'll soon be stepping in front of a microphone."

The school superintendent would not like that one bit, but there was nothing she could do. She was not going to let this jerk get away with what he'd done to her and countless others.

In fact, the law might get involved once he was revealed.

"All right, just keep me posted."

"No leaks, Emily. If the owners get wind of what we've learned, they will block us at every turn."

"Of course," she said, knowing the owners already knew of his sexy shenanigans. "Any inquiries into me playing on another team?"

There was silence for a moment.

"I'm sorry, nothing," he said. "Maybe after this breaks and they learn the truth."

"Maybe," she said. "Doubtful, and if I'm not careful, the high school I'm at will fire me. Already a jerk has leaked my story to the local paper."

"Damn," the lawyer said. "Until this story breaks, you can't talk to anyone."

"I know," she said. "Instead it looks like the town is going to paint me to be some Jezebel. Have I ever told you I don't like being the center of attention, especially in regard to my sex life?"

The lawyer chuckled. "Yes, the first time we met. Hang in there. After we get through with this, you may never have to work again."

But that wasn't what she wanted. She loved her job. She loved basketball, and all she'd wanted was to be a good player. A team player. Even being a coach made her happy.

"I'll call you as soon as I know more," Allen said. "Thanks for getting back to me so quickly."

"Talk to you soon," she said, disconnecting.

Damn, she couldn't get a break. Not a single one.

The next morning, she walked into the gym at a quarter till six to get everything prepared for their first morning practice.

When she flipped on the lights, she stared at the sign she'd made for Zach. He'd found it before he drove off the parking lot. Dang.

Now it was hanging on her door. Quickly she removed it. Taking it out to the dumpster, she threw it in.

She was really hoping he would get to drive through town with it on the back of his truck, but that didn't happen. Oh, well, maybe it was for the best. All she needed was for him to file a grievance against her with the superintendent. They would have her all packed up and out the door before she could explain why she'd tried to let the town know of his actions.

At six o'clock about half the team had come stumbling in. A couple more came running in several minutes later, apologizing profusely.

One irate mother walked in at five after six.

"Who the hell schedules a basketball practice at six in the morning?"

"A winning team does," she told the woman not wanting to deal with her. "Now if you'll excuse me, it's time we got started. Center court, twenty-five jumping jacks."

The woman stuttered.

"Really? I'm going to call the superintendent on you."

"For what? Doing what he hired me to do? Create a winning girls' team?"

"No, for being rude and not talking to me," the lady said.

She turned and faced her. "What do you want me to say to you? I'm trying my best to create a winning team. It's my first week here and I can only have the court half the time, so I'm now using the court in the morning for the other half of the time. If you'd like to find me another place inside to practice at a decent hour, we can go there. But for now, this is all I have to work with."

The woman shook her head. "I hope this is worth it."

Oh, she had no idea how much Emily needed this to be worth it, for this team to become successful.

"It was for me," she said softly. "Now if you'll excuse me, I really need to get these girls warmed up and doing drills."

"Hey, aren't you that professional player—"

"Ma'am, I'm kindly asking you to leave. Not in front of my students, please," she said not wanting them to learn of her issue.

The woman sighed and frowned, grumbling under her breath that she was going to contact the principal about this.

"Get warmed up," Emily instructed her girls.

For the next two hours, her girls ran through the drills. At eight o'clock, she dismissed them. "Hit the showers, ladies, and have a great day. I'll see you later where we will work outside until five."

Glancing around, she picked up the paperwork that listed who had not shown up today. This afternoon, they would sit on the bench and she would give them the chance to change their schedule. One more missed practice and they would be kicked off the team.

Just then she saw one of her girls standing at the girls' locker room entrance. "Miss Martin. Can you please come here?"

She walked over to where the girl was trying to stand behind the door, so no one could see her.

"There are no towels in the locker room. None," she said.

Shaking her head, Emily knew immediately what happened.

"Don't worry, I'll find some," she said.

Going over to the boys' side, she hoped it was empty.

Walking in, she yelled. "Anyone in here?"

There was no answer.

Then she saw the pile of old spare jock straps and grinned. These were for the kids who left theirs at home.

Also there was a whole stack of fresh towels.

Picking them up, she shoved the jock straps inside one of the towels and then she hurried out the door.

Before she went into the girls' locker room, she took the boys' jock straps and stuffed them in her desk drawer.

Then she took the stack of towels into the locker room much to the relief of the players.

If Zach thought taking their towels was going to deter her, he was dead wrong.

As she came out of the locker room, he walked into the gym. A grin spread across his face and she smiled at him. "Good morning."

"Good morning, Miss Martin. Did you have a great workout this morning," he asked.

"Yes, we did," she said. "Today was the first time I saw some progress."

"Well, good for you," he responded with a little laugh.

That laugh told her everything. He thought he had the upper hand, but he was sorely mistaken.

"Thanks for the sign on the door. But I'm not the reject," she said with confidence. "Oh, and the boys' locker room is probably without towels. Seems someone took all the towels out of the girls' showers."

Shaking his head, he walked to his office. "Have a really great day, Miss Martin."

"You too," she said, thinking she wished he didn't look quite so good. Sadly, her body still reacted to him. Sadly, her heart still warmed at that tempting smile of his.

"Miss Martin, can I see you a moment?" It was the principal, Mr. Townsend.

"Of course," she said. "My office or yours?"

"Yours will be fine."

They walked into her office and he shut the door behind him and then sank into a chair.

Shaking his head, he laughed. "This morning I've already received two phone calls complaining that you made your team come in at six a.m. and practice today."

"Yes, sir," she said. "It's only fair that we share the center court with the boys' team. So I made the decision that on the days we are not getting the center court, we would come in at six and practice then. In the afternoon, we'll practice drills outside, but they need the inside center court practice every day."

The man sighed. "Riley Hall has been the star player for the girls for the last three years. This is her senior year and her mother was one of the ones who complained. Riley told her she would be kicked off the team if she didn't show up. Is that true?"

And Riley was also one of the biggest whiners.

"I'm trying to instill a team spirit in these girls. You would think that Riley would want that state trophy more than anyone since it's her senior year. But, yes, I told all the girls that if they did not show up, they would be put on probation. If they missed two team workouts, they will be kicked off the team."

The man laughed. "Plus, we've had several phone calls about that article in the paper. It's your first week and you're not fitting into the culture of Cupid High School very well."

Just what she needed.

"The article in the newspaper is because a fellow teacher alerted them that I was here. The superintendent wants a winning girls' team. His daughter is on the team. He said it was past time. I'm trying to use my skills as a professional to help these girls. And yet I have a teacher/coach, parents, and now possibly you, working against me. What is it you want me to do? I'm not a miracle worker."

Oh God, if he learned about the shenanigans being played between her and Zach, she'd be walked out the door.

"Miss Martin, you're new to teaching, and well, it's not an easy profession. Not that I'm saying being a professional basketball player is either. But you have to deal with the parents and faculty, and well, you've got a hard road in front of you. If you take the girls to state, you'll be a hero, but between then and now, it's not going to be easy. So I'll just say be careful about what you do. One little thing done wrong will have a platoon of pitchfork-wielding parents coming for you."

She feared they already were.

Standing, he shook his head. "The position you're in, I don't envy you. You're damned if you do and you're damned if you don't. Just remember, I will always stand on the side of the students. Always."

"Thank you for the advice, Mr. Townsend," she said. "Let's hope I last through the rest of the season at least."

He grinned. "That will be a miracle."

"Yeah, my thoughts too," she said as he walked out the door.

The thought of the jock straps in her bottom drawer left her feeling uneasy. Maybe she shouldn't do what she was planning. But then again…

# CHAPTER 5

Later that afternoon, Zach watched as Emily stood in front of her girls sitting on the bleachers. First, she showed them some new techniques and then she pulled up a video of the team they were playing next week and started going over the weak areas.

While he tried to pay attention to his boys' practice, he was drawn to the way she coached her girls.

Finally, at the end, she gave them a pep talk that he couldn't help but overhear.

"This morning everyone showed up but three. Thank you for committing to the team. Thank you for your willingness to get up early and prove to me that you want this team to get better. I'm going to add one more thing to your day and then you can hit the showers. To build endurance, I want everyone to commit to running three laps around the football field every day."

There were groans.

"Yes, I know, and I'll be out there with you just as soon as I take care of some business. I need to see Janice, Beverly, and Georgia. The rest of you run your three laps and you're free to go."

The girls rose, some of them snickering as they walked past the three troublemakers on their way out the door.

"Move down closer," she told the ladies sitting on the back row of the bleachers.

Already he could see that they were giving her attitude. One of them was the superintendent's daughter and he wondered if Emily knew.

"Ladies, you didn't show up for morning practice," she said. "Why?"

"I didn't wake up in time," Janice said with a sigh and a flick of her hand in a dramatic fashion. "I never get up before seven."

Beverly shrugged. "I had homework I needed to finish."

Georgia glanced at her, pursed her lips, and shrugged her shoulders. "Didn't want to."

Emily smiled at them. "Being on this team is your choice. All three of you will sit out the next game."

Sputters of protest came from the three girls, some of her best players. They knew they were good and she would probably lose the game if they weren't playing. But he could see she was determined to let them know they were not going to be in control.

"If you miss again, I will have you transferred to study hall during this time period. I'm building a winning team and if you choose not to be a part of it, that's your choice.

We will do better with or without you. Again, your choice. You're dismissed."

"I'm going to tell my daddy what you're doing," Georgia said, rising. "I'm going to get you fired."

Oh, she was a little bitch.

"Good. I'm sure he will understand," she said and turned and walked away.

From the distance, he could see that she was irritated, but he had to admire her courage. She walked past him.

"Good job," he said softly.

She didn't respond but instead went out the door to run around the track. It was the way she'd always cooled her temper. And he knew because he'd experienced that temper before.

Glancing back at his team, they were all standing there staring at him.

"Coach?" Jayden said. "You got a crush on her?"

"Laps," he said, ignoring them. "Tomorrow morning everyone at the gym at six a.m. We're going to start doing morning training. But, for now, everyone do three laps around the track."

Groans were heard, but he knew they realized the girls' team was looking better after their morning practice. Already he was seeing improvement.

As they filed past him on the way out the door, several gave him a sly grin. His biggest player passed him and winked at him. "She's hot."

"Six a.m.," he reiterated, ignoring the comment.

That was all he needed was for his boys to notice he

was attracted to Emily. Because then, the coaches would hear about it and he'd get nothing but shit from them. Shit he didn't need.

Thirty minutes later, the kids had all come back in and hit the showers. Emily's girls were gone and she was in her office.

Unable to resist, he walked into her office.

"Do you know how to knock?"

"Why? You doing something you shouldn't?"

"What if I was? After the way you stole the girls' towels and hung a sign up, it is payback time."

"You started the sign," he said.

"You called the newspaper," she replied.

He grinned. "Score."

"I'm just sad you didn't drive through town with it attached to your truck."

Oh, the damage had been done.

"Oh, it's even worse," he said. "A reporter told me about the sign and he was taking pictures. I can see the headline now. Two high school basketball coaches feuding at school. And then by putting the superintendent's daughter on probation today, I'm sure that's going to make him real happy. That article could be the icing on the cake that sends you packing."

She leaned back in her chair and smiled. "You'd like that wouldn't you."

Strangely, he didn't want her to go. He was enjoying sparing with her and she was not hard on the eyes.

"No, you've made the girls' team better. And Georgia

can be strong-willed."

"Yes, I'm expecting the phone call from daddy at any moment," she said.

"You were right to do what you did," he said. "The other girls will respect you more."

Slowly he stood from the chair.

"Gotta go. I'm doing some one-on-one teaching with Jayden. But I wanted to drop in and give you some encouragement."

"Thank you," she said. "So are you declaring a truce?"

He laughed. "Never."

"That's all I needed to know," she said with a grin.

Why did he get the feeling he was going to regret not admitting defeat and declaring a truce? Why?

For the next hour, he and Jayden practiced. He noticed that Jayden had a dark spot on his brow.

After they had done drills, he gave the boy a chance to catch his breath.

"What's that shadow on your eye?"

"I ran into a wall," he said.

How many times had Zach used that same excuse?

"When I was a boy that wall would come up and smack me so many times. I often wondered how none of my teachers ever saw it. But then I also feared what would happen if they did do something."

The kid glanced up at him. "He drinks."

"Yes, my father used to drink. I'm not going to say anything unless you want me to. But I'm hoping that by helping you become a better basketball player, you'll receive a scholarship and get out of that situation. That's what I did."

The boy nodded. "Agree. Let's practice."

His heart ached for the kid, and he was torn about whether he should contact CPS or look away. He even considered telling the kid he had a place to stay if he needed one.

At the end of practice, he had to say something. "Here is my phone number. If you ever need help, contact me. Don't let him beat you. For now, this is our secret."

"Thanks, Coach," he said. "I gotta go or he'll get mad."

"Good practice, Jayden."

The kid ran out the door and his frustration at not knowing what to do hit him hard. What if the man killed him like his own father had killed his younger brother?

The next morning, at almost six, he turned the key in the door to the gym and took a step inside. Something smacked him in the face. Something smelly with a gooey cream in it.

Reaching for the lights, he turned them on to see jock straps hanging from the goalposts, the door, and even his office was decorated with them.

The dirty jock straps that had gone missing from the locker room. He should have known.

Damn!

Glancing around the gym, he started laughing. This was good. Damn good. How in the world could he ever repay this stunt?

February was just a few days away. Maybe he could

convince her to do the Cupid run. The silly town superstition that if you ran around the Cupid statue naked, the first person you saw was the person you were meant to marry.

Why people believed in that crap, he didn't know.

Some couples in town swore by it. The local sheriff hated it. The town's coffers were filled with the fines the city collected from the people who thought they wouldn't get caught.

This might just be the end of Emily's teaching career, if he could get her to agree to dance around the statue without knowing about the superstition, then he could tell the sheriff and she would be automatically fired from the school.

Could he be so mean?

Did he want to end her coaching career? He'd been enjoying teasing and giving her hell. She made his days more interesting.

Yet every time he looked at her, he remembered their time together. The way her breasts felt in his hands. The little noises she made when they made love. The feel of her snug against his chest. The way they had laughed and loved, right up until that day everything ended.

Damn! He wanted her and that couldn't be good. Just the thought of seeing her with another man was enough to make him decide he had to do this. She couldn't stay or he would be destroyed.

The pain from their time together sat like a rock on his chest. She had chosen basketball over him.

He had to get even.

# CHAPTER 6

There had been no call from the superintendent and all three girls had shown up for the next morning's workout. Now three days later, she was preparing the team for their first game with her as their coach.

The boys' team had traveled yesterday afternoon to Mineral Wells where they played against the high school there. They had been defeated and today the atmosphere in the gym was a little down.

The kids seemed really disappointed and it was all she could do not to try to cheer them up. But that wasn't her place.

She had yet to see Zach and she couldn't wait to give him hell about the loss. And yet, she feared what her first game as coach was going to be like. Right now in the season, the girls were 15-9. Not bad, not good. They were in last place in their division with many more deserving schools ahead of them.

And as much as she'd like to end the season as champions, she didn't know if that was possible. But if they were invited to the UIL tournament, that would create a lot of buzz.

With only eleven games left, they would need to win all of them to advance. She just didn't know if that was possible.

The boys' team was hanging on by a thread in their division and last night's loss was not going to help.

"Georgia, protect the ball," she yelled as she watched her girls practice.

"Beverly, a six-year-old could get by you. Guard, use your arms, your hands, your body."

Blowing her whistle she brought the play to a stop.

"Their team is known for stealing, if you don't protect the ball with your body, they're going to take it away from you. Twist away from your opponent. Grip the ball tightly and always be searching for the next move to the basket, even if it's not you. Now let's try again," she said, walking backward to the edge of the court.

She bumped into a hard male body and knew instantly from the touch of his hand on her arm who had stopped her from falling.

"Going somewhere?" he asked softly in her ear.

This wasn't good. Not in front of her team.

She whirled around and stepped away from him. "Zach."

Gazing at her, his face seemed concerned.

"Meet me at the Cupid grill at six o'clock," he said.

"You're asking me to dinner? Right here in front of everyone."

"No, I'm telling you to meet me there. We need to talk without prying eyes and ears."

What was going on? Why would he want to talk to her?

"What's this about?"

For a moment, he shook his head. "It's not a date. It's a chance for us to talk. Unless you want me to take all the greased jock straps and hang them in your office, be there."

A smile spread across her face.

"I thought you would enjoy the jock straps," she said, turning back to the court. "Janice, block her or she's going to run over you."

He leaned in and she could smell the mixture of manliness and sweat. He'd been outside working with his boys and while it was only the end of January, the Texas sun could be warm.

A trickle of awareness spiraled through her as she breathed deeply.

"Are you coming?"

Oh, there were so many responses she could make to that comment, but it wouldn't be appropriate. A big smile crossed her face.

"I'll be there," she said as she flipped her hair back. "Now go on, you're interrupting my practice."

What was she doing agreeing to meet him someplace to talk? She'd given the man the opportunity to end this dangerous game they were playing, and he didn't seem to want to stop.

And now he was asking her to dinner? He said it wasn't a date, but her Spidey senses were all a tingle clear to her center. And actually, she would have been so happy if he asked her to dinner as a date.

Something was up.

Suddenly there was a scream as two of the girls ran into each other and ended up falling on the floor.

"Watch where you're going, bitch," Beverly said, jumping up and standing over the smaller girl. Already she'd learned that Beverly could be a bully.

Alice was the sweetest girl, and she was lying on the floor, holding her head.

Emily made her way to the girl, who was trying to sit up.

"Are you all right?"

"Yes," the girl said with a sigh.

"You tripped her," Jessica, one of the strongest members of the team, said. "Why are you trying to injure your own teammates?"

Crap, she hadn't seen what was going on because Zach had distracted her.

"Stop," she said. "We're a team. We don't hurt each other. I didn't see what happened, but Beverly if you deliberately tripped her, I will bench you for the rest of the season. We support one another and play together. We help each other."

"She can't play," Beverly said in a whine. "She's terrible."

Oh, if only Beverly knew how close to being benched she was. And she shouldn't be bragging about her talents because she was a good blocker and that was it. She couldn't hit a basket if was held right in front of her.

"Alice is a good player, and every day, she's getting better. She's focused and knows the goal is to win the next eleven games. Every day, all of you are getting better."

Beverly gave a little laugh and threw up her hands.

"Not possible with these girls," the know-it-all teenager said.

"Help your teammate up and apologize," Emily demanded. If the girl didn't, she wouldn't be playing again. Second time in a week.

The girl glared at Emily and then yanked Alice up.

"I'm sorry," she said in a patronizing voice.

That was all Emily could take. "Go. Hit the showers, Beverly. That's enough for the day. The rest of you continue."

They would be having a private chat while the other girls were in the shower.

Thirty minutes later, she released her players and sighed tiredly as they headed toward the locker rooms. Beverly had not come out and she was waiting to speak to her. She walked inside the locker room and was shocked to see everyone's clothes all piled into one big pile with soap squirted on them.

"What the hell?" Jessica said throwing up her arms. "Who did this?"

"Beverly," Alice said softly.

Emily didn't have the heart to admonish her for her language because she was thinking the same thing. Walking over to the pile, the girls were rummaging around trying to find their clothes.

Emily clenched her fists, her chest throbbing in anger. Zach wouldn't do this to her girls, but she would ask him about it just in case. But she didn't believe for a moment that he had done this.

Beverly was nowhere to be found.

"Ladies, if I ever learn that any of you were a part of this, you'll not be playing basketball with the team any longer. I'm not going to accept this kind of behavior," she said, feeling like a hypocrite.

Wasn't this exactly what she and Zach were doing to one another? But that was going to end tonight. If he wouldn't call a truce, she would.

Time to be a better person and end their perverse games.

Going to her office, she found Beverly's home phone number and called her mother.

"Hello," a woman said.

"Mrs. Anderson, this is coach Emily Martin. I'm calling about your daughter Beverly," she said.

"She's not here," she replied way too quickly. "Hey, are you that coach that got kicked off the team for being a whore? Why in the hell they hired you is beyond me. You're a slut. You broke up some family home with your sleeping around."

"Mrs. Anderson—" She tried to interrupt her, but the woman was not having it.

"I'm going to get you fired," she said. "You need to be aware that we're having a meeting and we're going to run you out of town."

It was all Emily could do not to respond to ask if they were going to use pitchforks and what happened to *innocent until proven guilty*.

"Get in line," she said. "Your daughter acted up in practice today and I was hoping to speak to you about it."

The woman laughed.

"My daughter doesn't do anything wrong compared to you. This is your fault because you can't control these girls."

Immediately, she understood there would be no reaching this woman. No matter what she said, Emily would be wrong and Beverly could have burned the place to the ground and it would be all right.

"Well, I just wanted to tell you that she piled all the girls' clothes in the middle of the locker room and squirted soap on them all. This is what she did to her teammates."

The woman laughed. "Beverly is very strong-willed. She must have thought those girls needed to wash their clothes. Don't worry about it because you're not going to be her coach much longer."

The woman hung up the phone.

Putting her head in her hands, Emily sighed. What made her take this job? Her love for the game. Maybe she should have just waited until everything blew over and then tried to find a team to coach. Right now, the score felt like the manwhore Michael Devans had twenty-one points while Emily had three.

Beverly would be benched. Maybe permanently.

A knock sounded on her office. She glanced up to see Brian standing there with a big welcoming smile.

"Can I help you?" she asked.

"You looked like you could use a friend," the man said. "I'm a good listener."

Oh no, she wasn't going to fall for that line.

He had not spoken to her since they were introduced, but here he was offering to be her friend. After her last encounter, she felt nervous whenever a man came into her office.

"What can I do for you, Coach?"

The sooner he got out of here, the better.

"A group of us are going down to the Cupid bar and we thought you might like to join us. We'll drink a few beers, dance a little, and then go home," he drawled.

There was something about the way he hesitated between *then* and *go home*. She wasn't trusting. Maybe it was innocent, but she had to be careful.

"Thank you for inviting me, but I've already got plans for tonight," she said and it wasn't a lie.

The man frowned. "Well, we go there quite often. You'll have to join us."

He leaned over her desk and ran his hand down her arm and she jerked back a trickle of fear spiraling down her spine.

Oh no, she was not going to get anywhere near this guy.

"Excuse me," she said. "I know you're married, and contrary to a popular misconception, I'm not into married men. Get out of my office or I will hit the panic button beneath my desk."

He jerked his arm back. "I was just trying to be friendly."

"Well, I'm not. Now leave," she said in a very fierce manner.

After the last attempt, she'd taken some self-defense classes and knew being stern and direct was the best way.

Brian turned and walked out the door, but she feared what he would do next. She'd hurt his male pride and men like him got even.

Immediately, she sent an email to the principal.

Her desk phone rang.

"Miss Martin, you are becoming quite the challenge," Mr. Townsend said.

"I'm sorry, sir, really I don't want to be," she replied.

"I had just hung up with Mrs. Anderson," he said.

"Oh, no," she replied. "Well, she said she was going to get me fired."

The man laughed. "Her daughter, Beverly, stays in trouble. I should have warned you. Her mother and I have weekly conversations."

"So I don't need to pack up my desk," she said.

"Not yet. But let me know if Coach Brian becomes a problem. He's been written up once before. A second time will get him fired. Are you going to file a harassment report?"

She sighed. "If I did, it would only confirm what people believe about me. No, sir, but I wanted someone else to know in case this got out of hand. Honestly, I just want to coach or play basketball. That's all."

"And I just want to retire," he said. "Leave the crazy parents and the faculty to someone much younger."

She grinned. She really did like the man.

"Have a nice evening, Mr. Townsend," she said into the phone. "I'm really trying not to cause trouble."

"I know," he replied. "You, too, have a restful evening."

Standing, she grabbed her coat and headed out the door. After a day like today, she was tempted to order a glass of wine at dinner, but she didn't know if that would be appropriate. And she wondered what Zach had to say.

All she really wanted to do was go home or to the gym and work out, but she promised him she would be there, so she was going.

# CHAPTER 7

Zach sat waiting for her, hoping she would not stand him up. He'd overheard some things at school today and he was concerned for her safety. Some of the other coaches were banding with some parents and they planned on setting her up.

Why anyone would want to poke the auburn-haired beauty was beyond him. Didn't they know redheads had a temper? Didn't they know that if you poke the bear long enough, eventually, he comes out fighting?

Why not give Emily a chance?

Sitting at a table, he glanced around at the people in the restaurant and worried that someone he knew was here or someone from the press. Being seen with Emily in public was risky.

Maybe it was time he took a chance.

When she walked in, she had changed and was wearing a nice pair of jeans and a sweater that made her blue eyes sparkle, and her auburn hair lay in curls down her back. A groan escaped him.

What the hell was he doing?

If ever he was playing with lighted matches, this was the time. And those matches could create an inferno and burn him to a crisp. All it would take was one touch and he'd be lost.

Standing, he motioned her over to their table and the entire restaurant seemed to stop and gaze at her. How could a woman this beautiful be such a talented basketball player?

"Hi," he said, pulling out her chair.

Everyone in the restaurant would believe they were on a date, but this was not a date. This was him telling her what he heard today. Warning her and then springing the trap for the cupid run.

Part of him hoped she wouldn't fall for his ploy. Part of him wanted her to know what this meant and to not accept his challenge.

"How are you?" he asked.

She sighed. "If I didn't love the game so much, I would walk out of this school. But the kids, most of them, I really enjoy teaching. Then there are the little princesses, who I could do without."

He grinned. The boys were the same way, but they weren't princesses. "I have trouble with a couple of the boys. My problem is they want to be the big, strong jock that everyone looks up to. They want to be the star player. And my two strong jocks can't dribble."

She laughed.

From across the table, he could smell her sweet perfume and he'd always enjoyed that flowery fragrance she wore. It was like breathing sunshine.

"Do you have problems with some players picking on others?"

"Yes," he said, remembering the fight he had to break up recently.

"Right after you left, Beverly tripped Alice and took her down. I sent her to the locker room and she took all the girls' clothes, piled them on the floor, and poured soap over them," she shook her head. "Unless, of course, that was you."

"No, it wasn't me," he said. "I would never involve the students in our little game, except for the towels. But never their clothes."

"Thank you," she said.

The waitress walked up to their table.

"Hello, Zach," she said.

The waitress turned to Emily and smiled. "You must be the new coach. I'm Taylor Jones. I'm married to the sheriff."

The woman had a pregnancy bump and Zach was happy for her and Ryan. They had all gone to school together here in Cupid.

"I'm Emily Martin," she said.

"Welcome to Cupid. I hear you're coaching the girls' basketball team," she said.

"Yes," Emily replied.

"What would guys like to drink?"

"Would you like to share a bottle of pinot grigio? Remember how we liked to drink that wine in college?" Emily said.

He'd forgotten and he did remember how much they enjoyed splitting a bottle between them. They were younger and walked home from the restaurant, so it was no big deal.

"I think I just want a glass," he said.

"That's probably for the best," she replied, gazing at him the way she used to look at him. The look that always made his heart do summersaults while his blood rushed through him, heating him all the way to his toes. Today was no different.

They ordered the wine and he told Taylor they would order dinner when she returned.

"You enjoyed Italian food and they have some really good dishes here," he told her.

"Remember that time we tried to cook Risotto and it tasted awful," she said, laughing.

He did remember that and all the good times they had together. The way they played, laughed, and teased until they found themselves in bed.

Damn! Why was he thinking of that now?

"Yes," he said, smiling at the memory of how hard they had worked on the dish, and finally, they had gone out to their favorite restaurant.

The waitress came back with their drinks and they each ordered the baked spaghetti. With a grin, she nodded. This had been their go-to meal whenever they were anxious about grades, classes, or even their favorite game.

After Taylor took their order, she smiled at him. "We've played some pretty good tricks on each other, but I'm calling a truce."

Damn! Why now?

"I'm in a very precarious position and expect to be fired at any moment. I'd hate to somehow implicate you and drag you into my world. In a couple months, after basketball season is over, things hopefully will change, but not now."

What was she referring to? What did she expect to change?

"You're probably right. But the reason I asked you here tonight was because I overheard something that you need to be aware of," he said, dreading telling her. "The coaches are going to ask you to go to the local bar with them. There will be a group of parents there who will confront you. The coaches were going to sneak out and leave you to fend for yourself."

A visible shiver rippled through her.

"Thank you for telling me," she said. "Brian asked me to go with them tonight, but I turned them down because I was coming here to meet you, and I don't go anywhere with married men without their wives present."

He couldn't blame her for that after what happened that got her fired. It was all he could do not to ask her about her relationship with the man in the front office, but he doubted she would tell him, and he didn't want to make her distrust him.

His conscience pricked at him as he wanted to get her to run around the Cupid statue. It would be all he could do to speak to Brian tomorrow at school. How could the man be involved in trying to bring down another coach?

Even Kyle and Cody had been a part of this plan, and he'd found it disgusting. Max refused, telling them they were cruel.

Now he really felt like a traitor. Wasn't that what he was doing? Trying to get her fired?

Suddenly, he didn't want to harm Emily.

"I was really disappointed in how Brian acted tonight," she said, "but let's not talk about that. Let's talk about what happened after you left college. Where did you go? You know I looked for you."

She looked for him? Why?

With a sigh, he gazed at her and drank his glass of wine. What the hell was he doing here? And why did it feel so right?

"After you told me that you were leaving to join the Seattle Miners, I made the decision to go find my destiny. My classes were finished and there was no one to watch me walk across the stage. So I left. I spent the summer attending basketball camps and trying to earn a spot on a professional team. I traveled across the country and saw much of the U.S. until I realized that no one was going to hire me to play professional ball. Then I started looking for a job as a coach. I was shocked when I was accepted here in Cupid. Mr. Townsend hired me."

She twirled her wine glass.

"I searched for you. I called you. I did everything I could to find you," she said. "You leaving left me devastated."

Shocked, he stared at her. What did she expect? She clearly chose basketball over him. Why was she so shocked at his leaving?

"After I received the contract, I had hoped we could work something out," she said. "I hoped that you would go with me to Seattle."

Sudden anger rushed through him. "You never said that," he told her. Now she was going to blame this on him?

"That's because you left," she responded. "You walked out and I never saw you again. When you learned I made the pros and you didn't, you were furious with me."

That was true, but it wasn't because she was offered a professional team. It was because she never mentioned the two of them going somewhere together. Suddenly, she was making plans on where to live and how to get her stuff there and nothing was said about him joining her. Nothing.

"You never asked me to join you," he said, his voice tense.

"Yes, I did," she replied. "You ignored me. It was like you were so angry at me, a woman had made it and you hadn't. When I said something about us going together, you never responded. And then you were gone. What was I supposed to think?"

It was true that he'd been livid. Not because her dream was coming true, but because he was not good enough. The poor boy from the wrong side of the tracks had once again been left out in the cold. The big leagues didn't draft him, but they had Emily.

But he didn't remember her ever asking him to go with her. Never.

"I don't believe you," he said.

"Of course, you don't," she said. "Why didn't you tell me how you were feeling?"

Oh, yes, he was going to admit to her that he'd had his hopes and dreams destroyed when he wasn't drafted. She was riding high and he was in the depths of despair. Those really didn't go together well.

Just then the food was delivered and the atmosphere at the table had gone from friendly and cordial to stifled. It was all Zach could do not to ask for a to-go box and leave.

So how was he going to get her to accept his Cupid challenge? After this conversation, he was once again ready to give her a very short coaching career.

"How's your food?" he asked, trying to control the anger coursing through him.

"Delicious," she responded. "So I guess now you're mad at me again?"

He gave a little chuckle. "Never was mad at you to begin with."

"Bullshit," she said.

The woman was direct.

"No, I was upset because I thought you were leaving me," he said. He didn't mention to her that he had already purchased the engagement ring and set up where he would propose to her.

He didn't mention that he hoped they would both be drafted and have to decide which team they were going to play on.

And then she got her offer and that was the end of that.

"I wanted you to go with me," she said softly.

So softly that he wanted to upend the table and go roaring out of the restaurant. It had to be a lie. It had to be.

Time to change the subject or he was going to leave.

"What have you done besides play basketball these last five years? Why haven't you married?"

Her brows rose as she gazed at him, her blue eyes piercing. "I was busy practicing, playing, and traveling with the team. Doing events with the team. My schedule was always arranged by the front office. No time for a relationship."

No time for him.

Oh, yes, it was time to finish what he'd started.

"I've got a challenge for you," he said. "If your girls lose the next game, you run around the Cupid statue at midnight. It's our town's little superstition, and supposedly, the first person you see is the person you're going to marry," he said.

She gazed at him, her blue eyes twinkling. "Sounds rather corny."

Oh, she had no idea.

"It is," he said. "But many people swear by it."

"Why would you want me to do this?"

"Because I don't think your girls are going to win and then we can all come out and laugh and watch you do the Cupid Dance."

"So you want to make fun of me," she said.

"No, it's just a bet. Nothing else."

She thought for a moment. "And if your boys lose, I think you should have to do the Cupid Dance."

His boys were playing the worst team in their division. They were going to win, so he wasn't worried. And yet they had lost against Mineral Wells the other night.

"All right," he said, feeling confident.

"What happens if we both win?" she asked.

That wasn't going to happen. He knew her girls were not good enough. They were playing a much better team in their division and they had lost the last three games. They were losers.

Even with Emily as their coach, they were losers.

"If we both win, we both have to do the Cupid Dance," he said, just throwing it out there, knowing there was a snowball's chance of them both winning.

"Deal," she said.

He grinned at her. She had no idea that she would be running naked.

And he planned on letting the students know and the paper as well. Coach Emily would be fired and his life could return to the boring normal it had been before she came to Cupid.

"The first person I see after I do the Cupid Dance is who I'm supposed to marry?"

"Yes," he said. "And it won't be me."

"Good," she replied. "We obviously don't do very well communicating. Because I wanted you to come with me. I wanted you there by my side. If you'd been there, that asshole…"

She motioned for the waitress to come over.

"Can you get me a to-go box and my bill?"

"All right," she said.

"You're not going to finish your meal?"

"I need to go," she said. "The wine has loosened my tongue and if I stay, I fear me letting the good people of Cupid see how angry I was at your leaving. How abandoned I felt. How…"

She closed her eyes, sighed, and then opened them again and smiled. "Zach, I wish you nothing but the best. May you find the love of your dreams and have everything you want."

It was like she was breaking things off with him and they weren't even dating. Damn her.

The waitress returned with her bill. Quickly, she paid in cash, stood, and picked up the Styrofoam box.

"See you at school tomorrow," she said with a smile as she walked away.

Shaking his head, he watched her stroll out the door. She acted like he was the one who had wronged her. When in fact, she'd wronged him. Had she asked him to go with her and he'd just not heard her?

No, that would have been too simple. Too easy. But would he have gone?

Probably not because she was right about one thing. He'd been furious that she'd been chosen to play professional ball and he hadn't.

What was wrong with people?

# CHAPTER 8

Emily had not slept well last night, and this morning, she was at the gym before dawn. When she walked through the door, there were no signs, nothing to greet her as she turned the lights on and put balls out for the girls to use to practice.

All night, she'd thought *what-if*. What if she and Zach had gone to Seattle together? She clearly remembered asking him to go with her, but he'd been in a fog. An angry haze she thought with time he would get over. A rage that she didn't realize included her until later.

When she'd learned he had packed up and left town without even saying good-bye, she'd been devastated. It had been the best and the worst time of her life. Being drafted was such an exciting time, and she couldn't share it with the man she loved.

His abandoning her had knocked her to her knees.

With a sigh, she picked up a ball and threw it into the

basket. She moved from one side of the gym to the other, and every time she planted, the ball went into the net. Shoot, rebound, set, shoot, rebound. Over and over, she practiced the drill, trying to rid the disappointment from her mind.

The girls came into the gym, but she was in her happy place, making baskets, driving for a score. Winning.

When her arms began to ache she stopped. The team stood on the edge of the court staring at her in awe.

Breathing hard, she could see the admiration in their eyes.

"And that, ladies, is how it's done. Let's get started," she said, feeling better after last night.

For the next two hours, they practiced hard. It was their best practice to date and she hoped they were starting to see they were better players. Their skills had improved, but what about their attitudes?

"All right, ladies, we will meet back here this afternoon for one final practice before the game tomorrow. I'll also be showing you the film of this team one more time. Hit the showers and have a great day," she told the girls as they began to wander toward the locker rooms.

In the distance, she watched as the gymnastics coach walked toward her office. The woman had lived here her entire life and Emily hoped she had some answers for her.

"Lauren, can I have a word with you?"

"Sure," she said, turning on the lights in her office. "You're at it awfully early this morning."

Emily stepped inside her office.

"Yes, our first game with me as the coach is tomorrow and I'm a little nervous," she said.

"Understandable," Lauren said.

"As you know I'm new to Cupid. Can you tell me about the superstition regarding this statue in town?"

The woman laughed. "Honey, that statue is problematic. Supposedly, if you run around the statue naked at midnight, the first person you see is who you're going to marry."

"Naked?" she said, nerves spiraling through her. What had she agreed to? He'd known. He'd known and convinced her to run. While secretly, she'd hoped they would see each other.

"Oh yes," Lauren said, laughing. "The sheriff and the city keep our coffers full from people who are doing the Cupid dance at midnight and get caught. If you're a teacher, you're fired."

Tears welled in her eyes. That son of a bitch was trying to get her fired. And now she was totally boxed in. She wanted her girls to win. She needed them to get that boost of confidence that all their hard work was paying off. If they won, she wouldn't have to do the dance unless Zach's boys won. Then they would both have to dance naked around the statue.

"Are you all right?"

Shaking her head, she sighed. "I'm so tired of men taking advantage of me. He didn't tell me the whole truth. But, damn it, I'm going to come out on top."

Wisely, the woman didn't ask her what she was referring to.

"Don't do the Cupid dance," she warned.

Emily was a woman of her word and she'd agreed to the stupid bet. But that didn't mean she had to run around naked. Maybe she'd wear her clothes. Maybe she'd switch out the time. After all, she wasn't interested in meeting her true love and he wasn't either.

This was a ploy to get her fired.

Lauren nodded. "I'm so glad I found my man and I'm married. Today's single world is full of cornflakes and nuts. And you need to watch out for the male coaches. They've been conjuring up something wicked where you're concerned. I don't know the plan, but don't fall for it."

Oh, she'd learned the plan last night and she would not be going anywhere near the Cupid Bar with them or anyone else.

She sighed. "I just want to do my job, be a good coach, and be kind to my students and fellow coaches. That's all."

Lauren gave her a hug. "I know, honey. You're enemy number one right now, and I get the feeling the press doesn't know the whole truth. I bet it wasn't your fault."

Oh, how Emily wanted to tell her the truth, but she had to remain quiet until the lawyer told her it was all right. That day seemed further and further out of her reach. And every day, she doubted she would still be here once the truth came out.

"Thank you, Lauren," she said with a sigh. "I better get ready for my first class."

"Be careful, Emily," she said.

As she walked toward her office, she wondered how she was going to react to Zach. Last night, at first, it felt like old times. But now that she'd learned the truth, she knew he was still playing games. Cupid games.

The war was back on.

And, damn it, she was going to win this. Screw the truce. Screw trying not to cause trouble.

He wasn't here yet and she had time for another prank.

Taking a jar of Vaseline from her desk, she went into his office in the dark and greased every desk handle, the phone, and anything he would touch. Afterward, she returned to her office and began her day.

About thirty minutes later, she heard a loud noise.

"Yuck," he yelled.

She stayed at her desk, watching the video of the school they were playing tomorrow night, making notes, planning her game strategy.

Suddenly he was in her office, his emerald eyes flashing with annoyance. "I thought you called a truce," he said, his face red.

She smiled at him. "Good morning, Zach. I did. Is something wrong?"

"Yes, someone put Vaseline on every doorknob and desk handle in my office. That's not a sign of a truce."

"I'm sorry to hear that," she said, leaning back. "Someone forgot to mention that you have to dance naked around the Cupid statue at midnight. Naked."

He stopped and a smile spread across his face.

"You do and the sheriff is usually sitting in the park just waiting for someone to come running without their clothes."

"So you want to get me fired," she said.

With a shrug, he grinned. "Revenge is often mean and cruel."

She shook her head at him. "Have you ever watched *Beauty and the Beast?*"

"No, that's a girl's show," he said, frowning.

"You should watch it. You remind me of the Beast. A poor man trapped in an ugly body, captured by a spell because of his behavior. The Zach I knew and loved would not have done this to anyone. When you weren't drafted, you became trapped in this ugly beast body. Oh, and by the way, the only way he can break the spell is by falling in love. Good luck with that."

He stared at her, his eyes narrowing. She could see he was getting mad.

"Are you calling me a beast?"

"Yes, I am," she said. "Now if you'll excuse me, I have a game to prepare for."

He ignored her.

"If I'm a beast, it's because of you," he claimed.

She laughed.

"No, it's because you were so upset that I was chosen and you weren't. I had no control over that. If it had been reversed, yes, I would have been disappointed, but I would have been so thrilled for you. You were never thrilled for me. Never. Now, get out of my office."

She looked back at the video she had paused, but then she couldn't keep the words from coming out of her mouth.

"If my girls lose, I'll do your Cupid Dance, but you better be nowhere near if I'm running because I don't want to see your beastly, grinning face. You are not my forever man. Good luck with the curse."

A smile filled his face.

"There will be paybacks for the Vaseline," he said as he walked out of her office.

After he left, he was stopped by Brian just outside her office. There was a terse exchange between them. She couldn't hear all of it, but the last line stunned her.

"Bother her again and I'll tell your wife," she heard Zach say. The words only confused her. Was he defending her while trying to get her fired?

Warmth filled her and as much as she tried to dislike Zach, there were still feelings for him just below the surface. No matter what she said, last night she had hoped in some small way they could get over the past.

She couldn't help but wonder what would have happened if they'd stayed together, if he hadn't abandoned their relationship.

And, yet, were they a good match? One simple misunderstanding and they hated one another. But did they? Did they really want to wring each other's neck or was this just their way of trying to keep from growing close?

Last night had started great and ended badly. Had they both gotten scared?

If he made an attempt to get them back together, would she go along with it?

With a sigh, her fists clenched and she turned back on the video.

Yes, she would, but it had to come from him first because she feared he would laugh at her if she tried to make restitution. And wasn't that what she'd tried last night?

She'd gone there hoping to make amends and that had been doused by him not believing her. That was five years ago. Did it matter?

Maybe they were never meant to be together. But no matter what, she would always have a soft spot for him. A place in her heart of happy memories of the two of them struggling through college. Memories that left her filled with sadness. Memories that she wanted the two of them to last forever.

But now they couldn't seem to agree for thirty minutes. Once again, the games were on. And she was determined that this time, she was going to be victorious.

She was tired of losing. Time to change the rules.

# CHAPTER 9

Zach sat at the girls' basketball game and watched in awe as Emily coached her team. When the girls left the court at the end of the first quarter, she met them at the edge congratulating them for playing well.

And they were playing exceptionally well. Right now, they were beating a team predicted to go to the UIL tournament. A team in the running for state champions.

Her best player, Riley, had gone from being an adversary to hanging on her every word. One of the other little princesses, Beverly, sat on the bench, popping her gum looking bored and he doubted she would see any court action tonight.

The stands were filled with students' parents, faculty, and people from town and even the press. Before the game, the press had taken several photos of the team during warm-ups and of the coach on the sidelines.

One reporter was so bold as to approach her and she'd signaled for the security officer to have him removed, sending a signal to everyone that she was not to be bothered.

Over the last couple of weeks, he'd seen the improvement in the girls, but had no idea they were capable of winning against this team.

Right now, the game was theirs to lose.

He watched as she leaned in close to her girls giving them instructions. The memory of her silky auburn hair flowing through his fingers as he brought her mouth in for a kiss had him squirming on the hard wooden bleacher.

Last night had felt like old times when they had fun together until he ruined it. He'd even stepped out on a limb and told her what the coaches were planning. They had fun until he'd screwed it up and then took his misdirection a step further.

Watching her doing what she loved, he couldn't help but wonder if he wanted her back. Did he? Then why was he acting like a dick?

To salvage his pride?

Looking at her, he wondered if his pride was worth it.

By Friday night, they should know who, if anyone, was running around the Cupid statue. Today, when she told him not to be nearby if she ran, it made him question his decision. Did he want another man to marry Emily? Or was this his way of trying to lock her in?

A roar from the crowd alerted him to Georgia stealing

the ball and dribbling her way to the other end, where she leaped up and made the shot.

In disbelief, he watched as the girls' team hustled the ball better than his boys did.

They were going to win this game unless something happened. For a moment, he wondered how he could stop their momentum, but then shook his head. Maybe it was for the best that Emily not run the Cupid statue.

He didn't want to be the reason she was fired. The woman had enough working against her at the moment, she didn't need him giving her more grief.

There were two minutes left in the game, and the crowd's excitement was palpable. The Cupid High School girls' basketball team was about to beat a top contender for the state championship.

At the sound of the final buzzer, the auditorium went wild.

Emily glanced up in the stands at him and grinned. She held her thumb up. He shook his head at her, feeling excited for her as the girls gathered around her and she congratulated them.

The coach from the other school walked across the court and shook her hand.

It was then he noticed the national press had entered the gymnasium. They were taking pictures of her and the girls and suddenly they turned their attention to the top of the bleachers.

Some idiot kid was holding a sign that said "Go Home Adulterer."

Damn, why couldn't they leave her alone? With a sigh, he realized he'd helped start this when he'd told the newspaper about her. This was his fault.

Several boos were sent their direction and Emily glanced up. A frown spread across her face.

A sense of protectiveness overcame Zach as he stood and began to make his way toward her.

"Congratulations, girls," she said. "Tomorrow morning, you can sleep in, but we will have a wrap-up tomorrow afternoon. Now, everyone, get to the showers."

The girls were still excited as they made their way to the locker rooms.

As he walked up to her, she smiled. "Tomorrow night is your turn."

"Yes," he said. "Your team has improved so much. If it was the beginning of the season, I'd think they were a contender for state."

She grinned. "Yes, I've been trying to calculate how we could get asked to the tournament, but it's a long shot."

Just then a reporter thrust a phone near her.

"Miss Martin, how does it feel to be coaching a high school team instead of playing professional ball."

A frown twisted her lips.

"Excuse me," she said as she walked toward the locker room.

Several reporters ran after her and when she reached the door, she turned and smiled at them. "Gentlemen, this is a ladies' locker room. I'm very protective of my young ladies. The first man who steps in here will be arrested by the security guard who is walking this way. And I will, personally, land a few blows on you before he gets here. Have a nice night."

They all started talking at once and she turned and went into the ladies' room.

A laugh escaped him as he watched her disappear. But he wasn't going anywhere. For some reason, he feared that tonight someone was going to try to take advantage of her.

He decided to wait and walk her to her car.

Thirty minutes later, she came out of the locker room with her gym bag loaded. The girls had all come out one by one.

"I waited for you," he said. "I thought it would be best if I escorted you to your car."

"You want to be seen with the adulteress?"

His gut told him that he didn't believe what she was accused of. But he could see the tension and the hurt that made her beautiful face tighten. He should kick that kid's ass.

"What adulteress are you talking about? The Emily I know would never have done such a thing and anyone who believes the media doesn't know you," he said.

She stopped and turned to him.

"Thank you. That's the nicest thing someone has said to me recently."

Tears filled her eyes, and he feared that when they walked out the door, they would be bombarded with questions. He would have to protect her.

"Why are you being nice to me?" she asked. "Last night,

you challenged me to a Cupid statue run and didn't tell me you had to be naked. Today, you were here cheering on my girls, and once we walk out the door, your name will be linked to mine."

How did he answer that? Yesterday, he had mixed emotions about her when they met for dinner. Today, all he could think about was what if he'd made a big mistake when he abandoned her.

Could he have been in the wrong?

"Because no matter what happened between us, I never want to see you hurt. And these reporters are like vultures. Tomorrow we'll go back to playing our silly games, but tonight, I want to protect you. Keep you safe."

The words had flowed from between his lips of their own accord. Was he regretting his actions regarding Seattle? Even here in Cupid?

"Are you ready?" she asked.

For a moment, he thought maybe it was a signal. Were they ready for more? A chance to return to the relationship they had in the past? A chance to mend their broken relationship and try again?

"Yes," he said, taking her elbow. "Stay close to me. And whatever you do, don't respond to them."

She chuckled. "All they want to hear is how bad I am. It wouldn't do any good to try to tell them the truth."

That made him believe in her even more. Something happened in Seattle and he would love to know the truth.

He opened the door and the crowd surged.

"Miss Martin, when are you returning to Seattle," a reporter screamed.

With their heads down, he got behind her and pushed her through the throng. He wasn't worried until he saw the group of parents standing off to the side with their signs screaming *adulteress* and *not with my children*. And some of the worst sayings he'd ever seen.

When the parents saw them, they begin to march toward them.

"Get in the car," he screamed.

"Not without you," she said.

They weren't after him. They wanted her. To embarrass her enough that she would concede and quit.

"Mr. Rowling, are you having an affair with her?"

It was so tempting to scream back yes, but he focused on getting them to her car without being stopped.

The Porsche started with her auto-remote and the parents jumped back.

Quickly, she climbed in and he went around to the passenger's side and slid into the car.

Locking the doors, she shifted into drive and they moved slowly through the people. A sign struck her car and he rolled down the window.

"Stop," he said, "unless you want to be charged for damage."

She pressed the gas pedal and they took off, pulling out of the teacher's parking lot.

"Well, that was fun," she said. "Looks like the anti-adultery crowd is not going to give me any rest."

"Nope," he said.

"Where to now?"

He glanced at her and grinned. "Seattle."

She laughed. "What for? Remember, they fired me."

He sighed. "I don't know, it just sounded like fun. Maybe I screwed up by not listening."

"Is that an admission?"

"No, honestly, I don't remember you saying anything about Seattle to me."

Five years ago, it would have been fun if he'd not been so certain she didn't want him. Now as he looked back, he realized he'd had his head shoved up his ass very far. He'd been hurt and disillusioned and he'd acted in a totally irresponsible way. One that he now realized had cost him dearly.

But how did he fix what he'd done? How did he get her to realize that maybe they should at least give them a second chance? And was that what he wanted?

"Let's go get ice cream instead," she said. "A root beer float."

He grinned. It was their comfort food when they were in college. A place they went whenever they needed a pick-me-up.

A few minutes later, they sat in the car, eating their root beer floats.

"Wow, I'd forgotten how good these are," he said, watching the carhops roller skate from car to car. He noticed as she licked her spoon with her tongue, and it was all he could do not to groan.

"How many girls have you brought here?" she asked, turning to face him.

What could he say that didn't make him sound like a loser? The first year after their breakup, he didn't date anyone. Then he'd gone out with several women, and each and every time, he compared them to her. In the last year, he'd had two dates and both had been disasters.

"No one. I've had two dates this year and they were one and done," he said. "How about you?"

"No time to date. Did you think it would be like this when we left college?"

For a moment, he thought about it and then shook his head. "No. I planned on playing professional ball. That knocked the wind out of my sails and I felt like the ball had been stolen from me."

"Have you considered coaching a college team?"

For the last year, he had been interviewing with college teams and he hoped that this spring he would be chosen for one. Especially since his team here in Cupid had done well. Maybe not state-championship well, but they were holding their own, and he'd be disappointed if they didn't get invited to the UIL tournament.

"Yes," he said. "But first you have to prove that you're good at teaching high school ball."

Nodding, she lifted the spoon to her lips and licked the ice cream off. Oh, God, how he wanted to pull her into his arms and run his tongue over her lips and dive into her mouth and taste…

It wasn't going to happen.

"Your boys are doing very well," she said.

"And tonight your girls showed they have promise," he said.

"Yes," she whispered, staring at him. "We were always such good friends."

It was true. They had been

"So do you still consider me a beast?"

She laughed. "Yes. Until you break the spell."

The spell of falling in love? Glancing at her, he knew the only person who could break its hold was her. Could there be a chance of them getting back together?

Maybe they should run the Cupid statue. Maybe he should run right toward her.

"You do realize that if my boys win tomorrow, we'll both be running the statue?"

Turning toward him, she smiled. "Yes. I do."

# CHAPTER 10

Friday morning when she arrived at the gym, her office was completely covered in plastic wrap. She even had to break the wrap that blocked her from entering.

"Zach strikes again," she said out loud.

Brian walked by and grinned at her. "Great game last night," he said.

"Miss Martin, please report to the principal's office," a voice announced over the PA system.

Shaking her head, she feared what this mean. Congratulations, you won your first game and now you're fired?

"Excuse me," she said. "I'm being summoned."

The man grinned and she wondered if he had something to do with her being called to Principal Townsend's office.

As she walked through the students, many of them smiled. "Congratulations, Miss Martin."

There was a friendliness in the halls that she'd never experienced. It felt good, and she knew that if she were canned, she would miss this place. These kids. Her team.

When she entered the main offices, his secretary glanced up. "Miss Martin, go on in, he's expecting you. Oh, and great game last night."

"Thank you," she said.

When she walked in, he smiled at her. "Shut the door behind you," he said. With a sigh, she didn't get the feeling this was good news. "Congratulations on a good game last night. The girls are playing more unified than I've ever seen them. You're doing a wonderful job despite all the controversy surrounding you."

"Thank you," she said.

Shaking his head, his forehead wrinkled like he'd tasted something bad. "I wanted to let you know that enough parents have complained that the school board is going to hold a hearing on whether or not you are a good influence on the students."

Of course, they were. A sinking sensation filled her stomach. When would this ever end?

"Last night, you demonstrated that you're exactly what these young girls need. That's the best our team has ever done. We beat one of the top schools. I've also watched you over the last few weeks, and if this would all just blow over, you would be an excellent permanent addition to our staff."

What could she say? That it was going to get better? It wasn't. Any day now, she expected to hear from her lawyer and then the real fight would begin. But if she said anything, he might fire her now.

"Am I allowed at this meeting? Can I bring my attorney?"

He frowned. "You have an attorney?"

"Yes, sir," she said, knowing she had said too much.

"Why would you have an attorney?"

Licking her lips, she told him just a fraction of the truth. "I'm still negotiating a final settlement with the Seattle Miners and he's handling that for me. It might be good for the school board to hear his investigation."

The man seemed to sag with relief. "Good. It's not an attorney to fight the school district."

"No, sir," she said.

The man sighed. "For a moment you had me worried."

She grinned. "I have no fight with the district."

"Good," he said, picking up a pen and clicking it. "You may attend and you can bring your attorney, but I would caution you that people seem to lose their self-control when it comes to their children. Someone in town has painted you as an evil woman and they're going to protect their daughters from you."

Her parents were the best and she'd been lucky right up until her mother got breast cancer. Basketball had rescued her. Saved her in her grief, and even now, she thought it kept her from going crazy. And then while she was in college, her father had a heart attack.

The memory of those days filled her with sadness and yet she could understand why these people were protecting their children. Only she wasn't who they needed safekeeping from. It was men like Michael Devans.

She smiled. "I can't blame them for wanting to make certain that the people teaching their daughters are decent and moral. But I've always believed innocent until proven guilty. I was convicted in the news without a judge and jury."

There was little more she could say without divulging confidences that her lawyer said she had to keep secret.

The man nodded. "I'll have to agree with you on that one. The hearing is set for one week from today. You'll have time for a couple of more games between now and then. Show them that we've hired someone who is exceptional to teach our girls."

Sensing the meeting was over, she stood.

"Oh, Mr. Townsend could another coach be behind these parents? I've heard some rumors that some male coaches were wanting to make an example of me."

His brows raised and he clenched his fist. "Let me do some checking," he said. "I'm glad you told me about this."

"Thank you, sir," she said and left his office. Glancing at her watch, she saw she had time for one phone call before her next class.

Wanting to be certain she was away from prying ears and eyes, she ran outside into the teachers' parking lot and called her lawyer.

"Good morning, Allen, it's me. I know you're working so hard on getting this together, can you give me any idea if we're any closer?"

A truck drove into the parking lot and she turned her back toward it.

"I've got great news. I've found two more women, so we're up to five. That's enough to convince people that he has a real problem. I'm working on contracts for everyone and I plan on hopefully holding the news conference next week. We'll fly you out here to Seattle the night before."

The time for the world learning the truth was growing closer, but would it be soon enough?

"The school board is holding a hearing a week from today with the parents who want me fired because I'm an adulteress. Is there any way we can have this press conference before then?"

She was pushing it, and she knew it. But it felt like a dragon was breathing down her back.

There was a moment of silence and she didn't know if what she needed was possible.

"I'll do my best," he said.

"Thank you," she replied, knowing that it wasn't for certain. "Let me know when I'm flying out. I'll need to ask for the day off."

"Of course," he said. "Don't worry, Emily, we're almost there. Hang on just a little longer. This is going to be huge."

"Thank God, it's almost over," she said and disconnected the call.

Turning to go into the gym, she nearly ran into Zach standing behind her with a confused look on his face.

"Are you going somewhere?"

"Just a day trip to finish some old business," she said, hoping he didn't hear anything.

"Good morning," he said with a smile.

"Good morning," she said, thinking that things between them felt different since they had gone out for ice cream.

With a sigh, he handed her a newspaper. "I thought you might want to see this. On the front page, there's a photo of Georgia setting up a shot with another player almost on her back. The headline reads 'Cupid Girls Win Big Against Mineral Wells.'"

Pride filled her. "Can I keep this?"

"Of course, I bought it for you. But I will warn you that those damn photographers have a photo of the two of us leaving together. I'm sure the gossips will be wagging their tongues today speculating about us."

Just what she didn't need.

"I warned you," she said. "Let's just hope that no one connects us from college."

"Too late," he said. "There's a whole article about how we dated in college."

"Just great," she said. "This is turning out to be a stellar day. I started the morning off in the principal's office."

His eyes widened, but he didn't ask why.

"There will be a school board hearing about me a week from today," she said. His eyes widened. "Some parents want to fire the adulteress."

With a sigh, he shook his head. "I'm sorry."

"Yeah, me too," she said. "If they knew the truth, they would understand. But I'm sworn to secrecy for now."

He reached out and ran his fingers down her cheek.

"I'm sorry, Emily. If you ever want to talk about what happened, let me know. I'm a good listener."

Tears welled in her eyes as she remembered how he would sit and let her rant and rave and cry. When her father died, he'd comforted her. He'd been the rock under her, and she'd forgotten how he made her feel like she was the only thing in his world that mattered while she grieved.

"Thank you," she said. "We better get back in there before another reporter takes a picture of us."

Glancing around he nodded. "You're right. Plus, I have a game tonight."

"I'll be there," she said. "Oh, and by the way, thanks for all the plastic wrap."

A grin spread across his face. "You're welcome."

"I'm going in a side door," he told her as he walked toward the side entrance.

She nodded knowing it was for the best that they not enter the school together.

Later that afternoon, she sat surrounded by many of her players as they watched the boys play their game that would decide who would run the Cupid stupid.

"Miss Martin," Georgia said. "I owe you an apology."

"What for?"

"For not listening to you when you first arrived. I just want you to know that I think you're the best basketball coach I've ever had."

Emily reached over and squeezed the girl's hand. "Thank you. That makes me feel good. We've got a chance of being invited to the UIL tournament. But we're going to have to work extra hard."

The girl seemed troubled and she licked her lips. "You know my father is the superintendent and sometimes I hear things I'm probably not supposed to know."

Emily's ears perked up as she stared at the girl.

"I know there are parents who want to get you fired. That's not going to happen if I can help it," she said.

Oh no, what she didn't need was for the students to get involved. Oh, how she just wished this would all go away.

"Georgia, please don't do anything that will put you or any of the students in jeopardy. I'm hoping that the truth soon comes out and everyone learns at the same time that I'm innocent. That's all I can say about the situation."

The girl frowned. "These people are fanatics. Please don't let them run you out of town. That's what they want to do."

"Thanks for telling me, Georgia. I'm going to be all right."

It was true. No matter what happened, she was going to be fine.

Just then the other team scored. The game was tight with Zach's boys playing good defense but lacking on offense.

"Jack needs to get closer to his opponent," Georgia said.

Emily laughed. "Yes, he does."

The other girls around her giggled and laughed.

"Miss Martin, do you like Mr. Rowling?" Oh no, the

rumors were starting and she had to nip them in the bud now.

"Of course," she said. "He's a good coach."

They all grinned at her like they knew her secret. "Did you date him in college?"

She wasn't going to lie to them. If she did, it would hurt the trust she was building with her players.

"Yes, we did," she replied. "Now let's get back to watching the game."

It was the last quarter and the two teams were battling it out. Zach had said he expected an easy win, but this had turned into a dogfight. There were only two minutes left on the clock when he called a time-out and waved his boys to the sidelines.

She watched as he gave them directions and then sent them back onto the court. This was it. The final minutes of the game.

"They're going to give the ball to Jimmie," Georgia said. "Watch. He is big and tall and he will drive it to the basket."

Sure enough, they gave the ball to Jimmie, but he was fouled. The ref gave him three free throws. That would be enough to win the game. All he needed was two.

With five seconds remaining on the clock, the kid hit the first basket. She watched as he seemed to focus on the rim of the basket and *boom,* another shot went in. Then another. He hit all three baskets.

The crowd screamed as the buzzer sounded and the boys' team won their game.

Standing, she and the girls walked down to the center court where they congratulated the team.

Shaking her head, she gazed at Zach. “Two wins.”

“Yes,” he said. “Looks like we’ll both be doing the dance.”

She sighed, fearing what could happen. “If you get me fired, we’re done.”

Turning, she walked away hoping that none of the girls understood their conversation.

Tomorrow night, they would remove their clothes and complete three laps around the statue.

# CHAPTER 11

For the first time ever, Zach had wanted to lose a basketball game. But at the last minute, his team had pulled out a squeaker over a team they should've beaten handily. If he'd lost, then it would've been only him here freezing his buns off, getting ready to run around the Cupid statue. Instead, both of them were shivering in the early February night. And he was so afraid.

He didn't want Emily to get fired. Why had he ever started this? Why couldn't he learn from his mistakes? He had created a lot of problems for Emily, and after their last few encounters, he felt bad.

What he'd done, she didn't deserve.

In fact, he really didn't want to do this tonight. It was quarter to twelve and he'd like to be at home snug in his bed. But stupidly, he'd thought to trick Emily. He should have known that she would've learned the truth.

"I'm not getting naked in front of you," she said,

standing shivering close to the statue in her clothes. It was almost midnight.

Shaking his head, he was ready to admit defeat. "Look, I think we should call this off. If either one of us gets caught, we're fired. You've had enough publicity that this would just be the icing on the cake and you could never get another job in basketball ever again."

Rubbing his hands together, he approached her. "Let's just go home and call it quits."

"No," she said. "I'm not going to back down. We made a bet. We've been going back and forth at one another since I arrived in Cupid. Tonight is the end. Tonight is our last prank and if you pull another one, I will get you fired."

He laughed. "It's too dangerous."

"After this year, I've discovered I like living life on the edge," she said. "We're doing this. It's five till twelve. Go to the other end and take your clothes off. And no, you are not going to be the first person I see. We're going to test this superstition."

That was part of his problem. He wanted to be the first person she saw. The only person she saw running around the statue. He wanted her back in his life. He wanted them to go back to the way they were before he let his anger get the best of him.

And now was not the time to make this realization. Damn, why couldn't he have realized this weeks ago instead of now?

"Who is going to pick you up?"

"It's all arranged. Don't worry about me."

But he did worry about her.

Turning, he walked to the other end of the park that held the Cupid statue. Glancing around, he searched the area to make certain no one was nearby. Quickly, he shed his clothes, hoping that no one would steal his sweats.

He thought he heard giggling but wasn't certain. Maybe it had been Emily. Rubbing his hands up and down his cold arms, he did a little dance to keep warm.

This was nuts. He'd lived here for years and knew the dangers of dancing around the statue. Why had he thought this was a good idea?

Because he wanted to get Emily fired.

Saying a little prayer that they wouldn't get caught, he heard the clock strike midnight and began to run. A slight breeze blew and he realized that it was near freezing. They could get frostbite in little time out here in the park without their clothes.

"Crap, it's cold," he said, his bare feet touching the ice-cold concrete. Three laps and they would be done.

Shivering, he did his best to keep the statue in between them until he saw the flashlight coming toward him.

No. Just no.

Turning, he ran as fast as he could. When he rounded the corner, he slammed into Emily.

"What the hell are you doing?"

"It's the sheriff," he said, grabbing her hand. "We've got to get out of here."

He pulled her into the park, streaking from bush to

bush, his bare feet stepping on twigs and thorns as they ran.

"Nice junk you got there," Emily said, giggling.

"Shh, do you want to go to jail," he asked. Why did it seem like he was more worried than she was? But then again, she would probably be fired next week due to the parents.

"No, but can't I admire your junk?"

Of all times for the woman to notice his anatomy. And yet, a warmth filled him at the thought of her eyeing his body.

"Now is not exactly a good time," he said, darting to another shrub, pulling her along behind him.

The sheriff suddenly yelled.

"What are you kids doing?"

His heart slammed into his chest, freezing his already cold blood.

"Hi, Officer," a young male voice said. Relief filled him. Someone else was in the park.

"We thought we'd see if anyone was doing the Cupid dance tonight."

Dear God, that was one of his players. Glancing from between the leaves, he saw three boys and three girls. All of them basketball players. All of them on the teams.

"Shit, members of our teams are here," he said.

A groan came from her.

A voice called out. "Someone is running around naked. I found their clothes."

The students laughed.

"I'll bet we'll see them just any moment, now," one of his players said.

"You kids go home, now," the sheriff said. "If you're still here in five minutes, I'm calling your parents and having them pick you up down at the station."

There was a grumble from them, but Zach watched as they turned around and went back to the parking lot.

It was then that he saw the flashlights weaving out into the darkened park. Quickly, he yanked Emily down to the ground. Trying to keep them hidden, he pulled her beneath a shrub and covered her body with his.

Oh no. What a huge mistake.

She gave a little giggle. "You're going to get me fired and I'm freezing."

"I'm trying to warm you."

He wished he could say the same for himself. But his blood was pulsing through him like the spark on a firecracker. And he knew he was in big trouble. The feel of her breasts crushed beneath his chest, her silky skin sliding against his own, and his body remembered her scent and what happened between them years ago.

"Zach," she said breathlessly. "I can feel your..."

Unable to get her to stop talking, he layered his mouth over hers. It felt like coming home. Like he'd returned to where he belonged and he could feel his cock surging between his legs where it was nestled up against her.

It would be so easy to simply slip in between her thighs and for them to have sex right here. But this wasn't where he wanted to take her for the first time.

Oh no, they couldn't do this now.

The light swung out above them.

"Nothing here," a voice called.

"Hmm, I wonder where they went," the other voice said. "Well, we've got their clothes. Another donation."

The sheriff laughed. "I thought for sure we were going to catch someone tonight."

Their footsteps faded as they walked away and Zach released her lips.

"Damn, Zach," she said. "That was close."

"And we have no clothes," he said.

"No," she replied. "And I was just going to call an Uber."

He rolled off her and started laughing, his cock standing at attention. Even in the darkness, he could see it bobbing in the cold.

"What are we going to do?" she asked.

"Find something to wear," he said.

She laughed hysterically. "We're going to get arrested, aren't we? I'm going to get fired. The press will be writing scandalous things about me. I'll never outlive this. I'm done."

Slowly she rose to her feet and he followed her.

"No," he said. "We're going to beat this. How far is your apartment?"

"About two blocks," she said.

"Let's go," he replied. "Stay right behind me. Where are your keys?"

"I didn't lock up because I didn't think this would take that long."

"You do like to live dangerously," he said. "But this time, I'm glad."

They were about to leave the park when the sheriff's patrol car whizzed by with its lights on.

"Good, they got a call," he said. "Let's just hope it's not someone entering your apartment."

"Ha-ha," she replied.

He grabbed her hand as they looked both ways and then ran across the street, naked as the day they were born.

"My feet are freezing," she said.

"Mine too."

Suddenly she stopped and refused to budge. "Damn, you're the first person I saw after doing the Cupid dance."

He wondered when she was going to realize they had seen each other first. But he wasn't disappointed. In fact, he was glad.

"Maybe it didn't take," he said. "We only made it around one and a half times. Come on, we've got to stay hidden. Standing naked in the middle of the street is a free trip to jail."

They heard a car coming and skirted behind a trash can.

"I can't believe I'm naked with you on a street at midnight," she said.

A chuckle escaped him. "I will say that I still enjoy gazing at you."

"I know. You made that abundantly clear," she said.

A dog howled as they raced down a dark alley.

"Someone is going to call the sheriff, if we don't hurry," she said.

"How much farther?"

"Just a block."

They paused as they reached a second busy street. A group of high school kids drove down the street, the music blaring.

"Oh God, that was some of my girls," she said. "We've got to get out of here."

The car stopped at a light and the kids jumped out and ran around the car before getting back in.

"At least they're having a good time."

Had someone alerted the kids about them doing the Cupid dance?

"Did you tell anyone?"

"No, did you?" she asked.

"No," he replied, trying to think back. "Tonight is the Valentine's Day dance. I bet they are on their way now to dance around the statue."

Now she remembered seeing the flyers all over school about the dance this Saturday night. Thank goodness she had not been asked to chaperone.

"Wait. You said something in front of my girls last night at the game. They understood and because of the dance, I bet they're running late."

"Thank goodness."

"No, not thank goodness. Someone knows we were planning on doing this and the sheriff has our clothes. We're screwed."

Just then the car took off and turned down the road that led into the park. They ran across the street and into another dark alley. They were going to be lucky if they didn't get shot.

"We're almost there," she said.

Racing around a corner, he suddenly pulled her back behind them.

In the darkness, the sheriff was climbing up a tree.

"Damn cat," they heard him say. "Come on. I'm ready to go home."

"Did you find him, Sheriff?"

"Yes, ma'am," he said.

They were standing behind a dumpster trying not to laugh.

"Got ya," he said as he hurried down the ladder.

"Oh, thank you so much, Sheriff. I really appreciate your time in finding my sweet kitty."

"You're welcome. Good night, Mrs. Raffsberger," he said and went to his car.

"The sheriff is Ryan, the husband of Taylor from the restaurant," he said, trying not to laugh at the absurdity of the sheriff climbing the tree for a cat. But the lady was a widow and the kitty was her baby.

Sitting behind the dumpster, they snickered like two teenagers. The sound of a car pulling away had Zach sticking his head around the dumpster.

Just then, a rat scampered across the alley. A shiver rippled through Zach and he slipped his hand across

Emily's mouth just as she started to scream. Thank God, the sound was muffled.

She shivered with cold. "Get me out of here, now."

"Let's go," he said, pulling her hand. "What's your apartment number?"

"2030," she said, suddenly slowing down.

"What's wrong?"

"We're almost home. I'm glad, but I have to admit this was fun," she said, laughing. "I haven't done anything this outrageous in a long time."

"Let's not relax until we're inside your apartment," he said. Zach wasn't ready for the night to end. He wanted more. A lot more. Reaching her apartment, he opened the door and pulled her inside.

"Now, I can do what I've wanted to do all evening," he said as he pushed her against the door, his mouth covering hers, overwhelming her mouth, demanding her surrender to the kiss he'd waited so long for. Tonight had proven to him that he didn't want to let her go. He wanted her back in his arms and nothing this time was going to stop him.

Her arms slipped up around his neck and he pressed his hardened body into hers. She moaned that sweet little sound that he loved.

Their lips broke apart and he sighed. "Emily, I want you."

"About damn time," she said with a groan as she pulled him toward her bedroom.

# CHAPTER 12

Emily sighed and reached for him, knowing this was what she needed. She had to have him tonight.

Now!

Taking his hand, she pulled him into her bedroom, not wanting to think about the possible consequences of her actions. Tonight, he'd protected her, he'd shielded her, and done everything he could to get her home safe and sound.

Yes, she believed he originally did this to get her fired, but something had changed. He'd even tried to back out of doing the dance. And Heaven forbid, they were the first persons they saw when they did the silly dance. If the superstition was true, then they were each other's mates. Lovers. Intended ones.

Pulling him onto the bed, there was no hesitation as she moved her hands down his chilled skin.

"You're cold," she gasped as she touched him.

"Not for long," he said, his lips kissing her shoulder and her neck as he moved toward her mouth.

She wanted to run her hands all over him, and she wanted his hands to touch her everywhere. She needed to feel his fingers trailing over her body, touching her in intimate places, making her even more eager for him. Already, she felt that she could go up in flames at any moment.

Though it had been years, she remembered his body. The feel of his strong muscles beneath her fingers and how his cock filled her hands, strong and ready to take her. This felt so right, so much like she had come home to the man she loved.

And, yes, she still loved Zach. Probably never stopped loving him.

Her breathing sounded harsh, but she couldn't get enough air, she couldn't stop her racing heart, she couldn't control this urge for him to be inside her, the two of them joining as one.

His fingers teased her center, plunging inside her. "Zach!"

Only with Zach did her world feel like it was right. She curled her fingers around his strong shaft and he gasped.

"Oh God, yes," he said as he kissed her, his mouth trailing kisses down her chest, his tongue laving her nipples as he sucked and pulled them causing her fingers to grasp his head.

Slowly he wound his way down her body until he reached her very center.

"You're mine," he said softly.

She was stunned at his words. Was he committing himself to her? How could he do that when there were so many unanswered questions between them?

When his mouth closed over her core, she moaned as pleasure skyrocketed through her. Heat raced through her like an inferno. Her fingers found his hair, and she clasped his head. He lifted her hips until his mouth was firmly planted on her center, and his tongue did the most wicked things to her until her world began to spiral out of control.

Gripping the sheets, she cried out as he played her body like a well-tuned instrument, making it sing.

"Zach," she cried as his tongue danced over her folds.

Whatever thoughts she had were replaced with a blinding, urgent need as she felt the orgasm spinning toward her, causing her to moan as heat gripped her.

The explosion came swiftly as she screamed his name. "Zach!"

"Ride with it, baby," he whispered against her which only seemed to increase the pleasure. His fingers replaced his tongue as he drove them into her, finding her pleasure button and prolonging the heat.

Before she could catch her breath, he rose above her and slammed himself into her. The pleasure was instant, and she sighed, gripping him, holding him as he began to pull out to plunge inside her again. She grabbed his buttocks and pulled him even deeper into her.

"Emily," he cried.

She pushed and pulled on his buttocks as they found each other's rhythm. His mouth covered hers in a kiss that left her gasping for breath. Once again, she felt the pressure mounting inside her, and this time, they would both be carried away.

He lifted her hips until they were pounding away at each other, the rhythm building inside her until she felt that she would explode.

Gasping, it felt like she'd come home. That here was everything she'd been searching for. Here in his arms, she felt protected, safe, everything she'd been missing. Here completed the circle of love she'd missed, the heat, the pressure, and the feeling of desperate need that only he could create. She had to have him. She wanted him so badly. Since they met, there had never been anyone else. No one.

"I'm going to come," he cried as he gasped, plunging into her.

Once again, she let the passion overwhelm her and grip her as she cried out. "Oh yes," she said as she let herself go and the world tilted around her.

Crashing back to earth, he slumped on top of her, and she realized for the first time tonight, she was truly warm again. For the first time in years, she felt complete.

When he rolled off her onto the bed, she lay there, slowly coming back to earth. Why had Zach been the only man to make her world explode around her?

Why with him did it feel so right, like this was where she was supposed to be?

After a few minutes, he rolled to the side and sat up gazing at her. Even in the darkness, she could see his serious expression, his emerald eyes filled with what looked like love, but she wasn't certain.

"We need to talk," he said.

Oh yes, they most certainly did. Suddenly her cell phone rang and she knew from the tone that it was her lawyer.

"I'm sorry, but I have to take this," she said, knowing it must be an emergency for him to call her this late. "Please, Zach, understand, this is an emergency."

Jumping out of bed, she ran into the living room where her cell phone lay on the counter.

"Hello," she said, hoping that Zach couldn't hear her conversation.

"The press conference is scheduled for Monday morning at nine a.m.," he said. "I've booked you a flight out of Dallas at six a.m. this morning. I know it's early, but I need you to get here as soon as you can so that we can prepare your statement and practice the interview. The other women will be here as well."

"That's in less than three hours," she said. "It'll take me an hour to get to the airport."

Standing there nude, she felt the excitement fill her. It was almost over.

"Just do your best. If you miss the flight, we'll get you on the next available one. And tell no one. This has to be a complete shock. We're almost there, let's not lose our advantage."

"All right," she said, thinking the conversation with Zach was going to have to wait. She had no choice. Would he think that once again she was choosing basketball over him?

"I've got to get packed," she said.

"Wear something very conservative," her lawyer said.

"Always," she replied. "See you soon."

Disconnecting, she turned and Zach was standing in the doorway of her bedroom, a frown on his handsome face.

"Leaving?"

"Yes," she said. "I'm sorry. We need to talk, I know that. And no, I'm not choosing basketball or anything else over you. I can't tell you what's going on, but it will soon be clear. And Zach, no it's not another team. I'm staying right here in Cupid unless I get fired."

A frown crossed his face, and he shook his head.

"Why does this feel so much like last time? You rushing around trying to get ready to leave."

"It's not. I promise you," she said going to him. "After this, there will be no more secrets between us. I promise."

"What about your game on Tuesday?"

"I'll be back," she said not certain the school would want her to return or if they would fire her immediately. But this news would clear her name, so hopefully they would want her to stay.

"Please, trust me," she said. "And when I return, we'll sit down and talk. This is not a prank. This is real life and I'm going to kick it in the butt."

She could see he was uncertain.

"All right, but I'm nervous. It just feels like déjà vu all over again," he said.

"No, Zach, I want us to work. Believe me, I don't like jumping out of bed with you and leaving. I wanted more. Just give me a little time," she said, gazing at him and seeing his unease. But she had to get on the road right away. "I'll get packed and drop you by your house on my way out of town."

He nodded.

As she turned away, he pulled her back into his arms and kissed her. When they broke apart, he sighed. "Let's not screw this up a second time," he said. "I'll be patiently waiting for your return."

She smiled and caressed his cheek. "It's going to be fine. I'll call you and let you know what's happening when I can."

Slipping out of his arms, she ran and jumped in the shower.

Finally, everything was going to come out in the open and her name would be cleared. And those parents with the adultery signs would soon be asking for her forgiveness.

# CHAPTER 13

Monday morning dawned, and with a heavy heart, Zach went to school. Everything felt strange and surreal. And his heart was certain that once again, she'd jilted him for something he didn't even understand.

This morning he received a text from her to have his television on at eleven o'clock to ESPN.

Had she lied and been offered a new contract? Or could this have anything to do with the team firing her?

Her girls had shown up at six a.m. this morning and done their workout without their coach being there. He'd been shocked. The superintendent must have let them into the gym.

It had been the best of weekends and the worst, all because they had reconnected. And yet once again, she was gone.

This time they had made their intentions clear and she

promised him that soon, she would tell him what was going on, but that worried him.

And this morning when he walked into the gym, his clothes were lying on his desk and through the window, he could see Emily's clothes were also in his office.

Someone knew what they'd done. And whoever it was, were they a good person or someone who would hang them out to dry?

Brian approached him. "Congratulations on the win Friday night."

"Thanks," he said, really not wanting to talk to the man. After he learned what the coach had planned for Emily, he wanted nothing to do with him.

"Look, I know you got upset with what we were going to do to Emily, but I wanted to let you know that someone spread a rumor about the two of you dancing around the statue on Saturday night. Is it true?"

Could he have been the one who retrieved their clothing? Zach had felt certain that the sheriff had picked up their clothes. They even spoke about donating them.

But they were lying neatly folded on his desk and so were Emily's.

"Thanks for letting me know," he said, neither confirming nor denying Brian's question.

"Did you see anyone?" The man was still referring to him dancing around the statue.

"Yes," he said. "I saw a great game on television Saturday night."

The man laughed. "You're not going to confirm you

danced around the statue. Did Emily go with you? Is that why she's not here today."

The man was a gossip and he wasn't going to tell him anything.

"I have no clue as to why she's not here today," he said which wasn't a lie. All he knew was that she had flown somewhere. "But her girls came in and did their drills this morning. If I wasn't here, I'm sure my boys would just sleep in."

Just then the bell rang announcing first class.

"Gotta get to work," Zach said as he hurried to his group of students waiting on him.

The hour passed quickly, and the next time he looked up, it was getting close to eleven. His last class of the morning ended at ten forty-five, so he would have time to get to his office and turn on the television.

What was going on that she would be on a big cable channel? Would this get her fired here in Cupid?

Being back here had been great, but if he received the opportunity to advance his career, he'd leave in a heartbeat. And he had put in several applications at colleges around the area.

Just as his class ended, he made his way toward his office. Principal Townsend stood waiting right outside his door. Crap.

"Mr. Rowling, may I have a word with you?"

"Of course," he said and opened his door to let the man in.

"Good game Friday night. The boys were a little slow to get started, but they pulled off a dramatic finish."

At the time, he had wanted them to lose, but now he felt grateful their win pushed him and Emily together. Because of the bet, they had done the Cupid dance. And someone knew.

"Yes, they worked hard to come back," he said, wishing the man would leave.

The principal crossed his legs and glanced around the office like he was looking for some way to say something.

"You've been a great addition to our faculty," he said.

"Thank you," Zach said, knowing if he didn't leave now, he was going to miss what was happening.

"When you arrived here, I didn't think you would stay this long. Now I'm receiving inquiries about you from other schools. Colleges to be exact. Do you plan on leaving us, Mr. Rowling?"

With a sigh, he knew he should have seen this coming. The long hand of the clock moved toward eleven. He couldn't stand it. He had to know what was going on.

"Excuse me. I really want to focus on our talk, but there is something I must do. And maybe it will affect you as well. I've got to turn on ESPN."

The principal made a strange noise like he couldn't believe he was going to watch TV instead of talking to him.

Quickly he turned on the small television in his office.

The announcer quietly said. "This press conference was called with regards to Michael Devans from the front office of the Seattle Miners."

The principal gasped. "That's Miss Martin. What is she doing?"

"I don't know," Zach said. "We're about to learn why she's there."

Five women were sitting at a long table with a microphone in front of them. Emily sat in the middle.

"Good morning. I'm attorney Allen Rockford," a man in a suit said. "We're here to announce a lawsuit against the Seattle Miners. These five women were victims of sexual aggression and malicious behavior that the team owners knew about and tried to suppress. All five of these ladies were threatened if they did not sleep with Mr. Devans, they would be fired. He would find a way to lie to the press about them and their contract would be nullified on moral grounds. It worked every time."

The man took a deep breath and gazed into the camera. "Today, these women have come forward to tell their story. We are seeking thirty-five million dollars in restitution, plus the remainder of their contract money. We can prove the owners of the team knew what this individual was doing and did nothing to stop him."

He handed the microphone to Emily. Zach could see her hand shaking. "Good morning, my name is Emily Martin. I played the forward position for the Seattle Miners for four years. Last year, I was called to Mr. Devans's office to renegotiate my contract. At the time, I thought it wasn't up for renewal until this year."

She licked her lips and sighed. "When I arrived at his office, he locked the door, which I thought was odd. He told me that my agent would not negotiate with him which was a lie. I sat in a chair across from him and he told me that if I would sleep with him, my contract would be renewed and I could continue playing for the Miners. If I refused him, he would show the pictures of me coming into his office. He would say that I slept with him and our affair ended his marriage. When I told him no, he tried to force himself on me, but I hit him and ran out the door."

With the sound of reporters busily scratching their pens across pads, the murmurs, and the flashes of light, Zach knew this was a major news story.

The lawyer took the mic back. "Mr. Devans and his wife have been separated and living in separate households for over two years. His wife confirmed that he's done this before."

Two years!

The lawyer handed the mic to the next woman sitting at the table and she told her story. Only she had been coerced into sleeping with the man. And she'd still been fired.

The principal and Zach sat there mesmerized by the interviews. Of the five players, two had refused to sleep with him and three had given in. All five were fired and Zach wondered if the man knew the team was not going to resign these women and took advantage of their situation.

In the end, the lawyer made his final remarks and then the reporters fired off questions. He watched as Emily and the women answered the questions one by one. Some of them were way too personal.

Finally, the lawyer held up his hand. "That's all. We'll see you in court."

The women stood and walked out of the room.

Speechless, he and the principal sat there.

"Dear God, I better call the school board members. And you had no idea this was going to happen?"

"No," he said. "She texted me and said be sure to watch ESPN at eleven."

The principal stood. "Retirement is only a few short years away and it can't get here soon enough."

Zach chuckled.

"We'll talk later about the inquiries I'm receiving about you," he said and rushed out the door.

Brian came running into his office. "Oh my God, have you heard?"

He saw the television was still on and the reporter was talking about the significance of this new lawsuit and what it could mean to the Seattle Miners.

"You knew," he said.

"No, I didn't. She told me to have the television on to ESPN. Mr. Townsend was in my office. All the parents who called her an adulteress, I think they owe her an apology."

Brian's face turned a sickly shade of yellow. "I helped them. And now I find out she's innocent. But she's such a beautiful woman, I can see how this could happen."

Zach leaned back and smiled. He couldn't wait for when Brian and the rest of the coaches figured out what was going on between him and Emily.

Just then his cell phone rang. He glanced down and saw that it was Emily.

"Excuse me, I need to take this," he said.

After Brian walked out the door, he answered. "Hello, beautiful. Now I understand why you had to leave immediately."

"Oh, Zach, it's almost over. The lawyer told me he knows they will not want this to go to trial because they would lose big time. So we expect to settle very soon. And the best thing is my name is clear. I'm not what everyone thought."

The best feeling overcame him. "I never doubted that for a moment. When will you get home?"

"Late tonight," she said.

"Oh, there is something you need to know. Mr. Townsend was here in my office and I told him I had to turn on the television. So he knows, and I'm sure by now the school board and the superintendent know."

"Oh, dear. You would think this would exonerate me, but I have a feeling I'm going to be in even more trouble."

"I fear you're right. The City of Cupid does not like its teachers to be on the national news for any reason. And this is going to be a big story for a while. I look for the press to be at our doors this afternoon."

"Ugh," she said. "You're right. But I had been warned not to tell anyone what was going on."

As much as he could see that, he wished she'd trusted him enough to tell him the truth.

"I'm sorry, I couldn't tell you. I promise you, there are no more secrets in my life. I'm pretty much an open book."

Sitting there, he loved hearing the sound of her voice.

"Don't be surprised if your office has Vaseline on all the knobs tomorrow," he said.

She giggled. "We're not playing Cupid games any longer. We're done."

"Oh no, we're not," he said softly. "There is still one big game for us to play."

"What's that?"

"It's a surprise. Get home and I'll show you."

"It will be really late when I get in tonight. I'll see you at school tomorrow if I still have a job."

"See you then," he said, knowing he had to do something special for her. And this afternoon, he had practice with Jayden.

# CHAPTER 14

Zach was distracted, but he was doing his best to help Jayden. With every drill, with every practice, the boy got better. If he was not a senior, he really believed that next year he would have been his star player.

"Jump," Zach yelled at him.

The kid was a great defensive player and a good blocker. Sometimes Zach wondered if that was what his life was like at home.

Suddenly the door to the gym slammed open and closed.

"Boy, I told you I needed your help today. No more basketball." A big man entered the gym and stumbled toward the court.

He grabbed Jayden by the jersey. "Get your ass in the truck, now."

"No," Jayden said.

The man pulled his arm back to hit the boy and Zach flew in between them.

"Don't you dare hit him," he said.

"Get out of my way. He's my son and I'll treat him any way I want to," he said with a growl. "Get out of my way or I'm going to hit you."

Zach stood between the man and his son.

"I've seen the bruises on this boy. He has three more months of high school. Three more and then I hope and pray he gets a scholarship so he can get away from you."

The man growled. "He's not going anywhere but to work for me. My son is not going to college."

"Why? Because then you won't be able to control him?"

"Dad, please stop," Jayden said. "If you hit Mr. Rowling, then I will tell CPS what you do to me and the other kids. Do you understand?"

That made Zach even more suspicious.

"Your son is a talented basketball player who should get a scholarship. With his education, he could help his family get out of poverty. Or is your pride more important than helping your family?"

The man glanced at his son, his lip curled into a sneer.

"You choose. This game or helping your papa."

"No," Zach said. "Don't put the pressure on him. Don't you want your son to have a good education in life? A basketball scholarship will pay for his college."

The man growled. "You're like your mother. Useless."

Zach remembered the days when it did no good to

argue with his father. The man would never admit he was wrong.

"There is a place in town that can help you learn to stop hitting your children. If I see another bruise on Jayden, I won't hesitate to call CPS. Do you understand? Now, you can sit on the bleachers while we finish our practice. Then your son can help you."

With a sigh, he walked over to the stands and Zach knew for certain that this wasn't over. But hopefully it was the first step for the man to see he couldn't continue to abuse his children.

Jayden was nervous and Zach tried to coach him out of his stiffness. They were going to finish today.

At the end of the practice, he walked Jayden over to his father. Zach reached into his pocket and gave Jayden a business card.

"Here. If you can get your family to go here, they can help you. Don't wait. My brother died from my father beating him. Don't let that happen to your family."

Walking away, he felt the rush of tears. How many kids experienced what Jayden and he experienced? How many families were destroyed by an abusive parent?

# CHAPTER 15

Emily was exhausted. She had not gotten in until almost one o'clock and when she arrived at her apartment, there were reporters everywhere. She almost turned around, but then she decided that she needed her bed.

As she pushed through them, her neighbors were not very happy that there was so much noise at that time of the night. But what could she do?

Walking into the apartment, she sighed and sank down in her chair until she saw a very nosy reporter trying to peek through her blinds.

"Get away from the window or I will call the sheriff," she yelled.

The man scrambled to get away, and she knew for the next week, her life would be hell.

Walking into the bedroom, she saw the rumpled sheets. She had not even made the bed before she ran out the door. That was so unlike her and she remembered what she'd been doing before she left.

With a sigh, she got into bed and breathed the smell of Zach.

Where did they go from here?

Now he knew the truth. She'd told him that she didn't choose basketball over him. They had been playing games since she'd moved to Cupid.

Time for the games to end and for them to decide if they had a future. And she knew what she wanted, but did he?

The next morning, she had a call from the superintendent's secretary. "Miss Martin, before you go to school, the superintendent would like to see you in his office."

Crimany! She was being fired. For the second time in her life, she would be without a job, insurance, or anyone backing her. She knew she should've expected this, but she had hoped they would give her a break since none of this was her fault.

Getting ready, she took two big bags to bring all her things home from the school office. She would miss her team, the girls, the challenges, even the pranks she and Zach had played on each other.

Dressing professionally, she pushed through the reporters to reach her car. "Please get back, so I don't run over you. I'm not saying anything else on the advice of my lawyer, so you're wasting your time. Have a great day."

She pushed a man who had his phone in her face out of the way and climbed into her car. She started the engine and revved the motor hoping to warn them before she put the car into drive.

The reporters scattered, but she knew they wouldn't give up easily. When she returned home, they would be waiting.

When she arrived at the superintendent's office, there were more reporters. She bent her head down and hurried into the building where the secretary was waiting. She unlocked the door and then quickly locked it behind her.

"Vultures," she said. "They're vultures waiting to pounce on you."

Emily smiled. "I had to deal with them when I got home at one o'clock this morning."

"Oh dear," she said, gazing at her sadly. "They're waiting for you inside."

"Thank you," she said, taking a deep breath and walking toward her sentencing.

They would fire her, but she hoped that someone else would hear her story and agree to hire her either as a coach or a player.

Feeling like she was going to her execution, she knocked on the door and then walked inside.

Stunned, she saw Zach sitting there as well as Principal Townsend.

"Good morning, Miss Martin. Please have a seat," the superintendent said, pointing to the chair next to Zach. "I trust you made it home safely."

"Yes, sir," she said, not wanting friendly chitchat, but

rather for them to pull the gauntlet, chop her head off, and send her on her merry way.

"Zach and I watched the conference call yesterday morning," the principal said. "It was quite distressing to see how you women were treated. I'm sorry for that."

"Thank you," she said.

"Yes, I had to look it up on the internet after Mr. Townsend contacted me. You've created quite a stir at the school, Miss Martin."

"I'm sorry, sir. I was warned not to talk to anyone about the investigation my lawyer was conducting. I couldn't tell you," she said.

She shifted in her chair and glanced at Zach. "May I ask why Zach is here? He didn't do anything wrong."

They laughed.

"You two have stirred up more trouble in the last two months than any teachers we've ever had before. And yes, we know you dated in college. We didn't know that when we hired you, Miss Martin, but after we became suspicious, we learned the truth."

Zach tensed. "There's nothing wrong with two people dating and then seeing each other again."

The superintendent leaned back. "No, there's not. And both of you are fine coaches. Miss Martin has led our girls to victory and I'm still hoping for a state championship. Zach, our boys' team has done very well under you. I'm just sad to hear that you're looking for a college team to coach."

Emily's head swiveled toward Zach. "Really?"

"Yes, I was going to tell you, but I haven't had the chance. But I've had no offers, yet."

She smiled at him. "You'll be excellent as a college coach."

The principal cleared his throat. "You two have played pranks on each other for the last two months. I also learned that Brian Finestein was behind the adulteress signs and planned on leaving you, Miss Martin, at the Cupid Bar and Grill to deal with the unhappy parents. His contract will not be renewed."

"I'm sorry to hear that," Emily said. "But I also had to remove him from my office once."

The principal rolled his eyes. "You shouldn't have been forced to do that."

"After my first experience with a threatening man, I took classes on how to fight back. I will never accept someone harassing me again."

The men were silent for a moment.

"So why are we here? Are you firing me?"

"No," the superintendent said.

"We wanted to warn you both. You're being watched. We know about the pranks. We also have it on good authority that you both ran around the Cupid statue. Did you know the students came out there to watch?" the principal shook his head. "I wish they would tear down that statue."

The superintendent laughed. "That will never happen. They make too much money off the fines."

"Look, the eyes of the nation are on Cupid schools. You

are representing us and the pranks have to stop. The janitorial staff has complained about the Vaseline and the Saran Wrap. I don't know what's going on between you two, but you need to act like teachers who represent good, moral characters to our students."

Zach sighed. "I take full responsibility. I'm the one who gave her a hard time from the moment she arrived. I've been a fool where she's concerned and done some really stupid things. Blame it all on me."

Emily was shocked. "No, I took part in the pranks as well."

He shook his head trying to get her to stop.

"Let's just say that this would have never happened if I hadn't been such a stubborn, prideful man who let her get away five years ago. I'm determined that's not going to happen again."

What did he mean by that?

The two men were smiling at them.

"We just wanted to warn you that the students have noticed and it's time to get whatever this thing is between you under control," the superintendent said. "And Miss Martin, the school board canceled tomorrow's hearing. You were not at fault and should not be punished. Our parents need to realize you are a victim."

Relief filled her. "Thank you. And thank you for not firing me this morning."

"No chance of that," the superintendent said. "Unless, of course, you get caught running the statue."

"Who returned our clothes?" Zach asked.

The superintendent grinned. "My daughter. She went to the sheriff's office and convinced them to let her have them. Miss Martin, you've made quite the believer out of my daughter. Thank you. She's becoming a much better basketball player."

Emily grinned. "She's a delight."

"All right, you are free to go. We'll be at the game tonight and can't wait to see if you win," the superintendent said.

The principal nodded. "Have a great day and good luck dodging the reporters."

When they stepped outside, Zach gazed at Emily as the reporters came rushing up. "I'll talk to you later tonight after the game."

Disappointment filled her, but she knew there was no way they could have a conversation with reporters screaming at her and asking her questions, and at school, they would both be busy.

"All right," she said. "We'll talk tonight."

All day, she looked for him at school, hoping for just a moment to say hello. Talk about what the superintendent and the principal said to them this morning, but she never saw him.

Later that afternoon, her team arrived for their last-minute game instructions, and brought her flowers.

Georgia came up to her. "We watched the press conference and just wanted to tell you we're so sorry that happened to you."

Tears filled her eyes. "Ladies, I hope something like this

never happens to you. But I want you all to learn how to protect yourself." Wiping her eyes clear of her tears, she continued. "Now, we have a big game tonight. I'm hoping we will beat the number one team in our division and get invited to the UIL championship."

The girls gave a whoop and holler as she turned on the big screen for them to watch the team they were playing. She would stop the film and point out weaknesses.

"All right, girls, suit up, it's game time," she told them.

An hour later, she paced frantically in front of the bleachers. She had not changed into her coaching attire but wore the nice suit she had worn to be fired in this morning. Her girls were playing exceptionally well tonight and she couldn't be prouder.

The gym was packed with parents, teachers, reporters, and students. Their game tonight would receive national attention all because of her lawsuit.

At the half, she ushered her girls into the locker room. She noticed they were excited and giggly and even whispering amongst themselves and she wondered what was going on.

"All right, ladies, pay attention," she told them. "We've got to get better at stealing their ball. Georgia, I want you to take the ball from them more. Riley, get the ball to Georgia whenever you can because she's the tallest. She can hit the basket from almost anywhere on the court. You're all doing very well. I'm so proud of you. Now go out there and show them that the Cupid Girls are capable of playing in the UIL tournament."

The girls cheered and ran out of the locker room before she could do their chant. They were acting strange and she didn't understand what was going on.

"Miss Martin," Georgia said. "I have a question for you."

"All right, but we need to go. We have a game to play," she told the girl.

"Are you in love with Zach?"

How did she answer this? Of course, she was in love with him, but did she want her team to know? She was tired of trying to hide from the truth. It was time to be honest.

"Georgia, yes, but we're working through some things," she said.

"Good," she said. "Come on."

The girl took her by the arm like she was escorting her and she was kind of surprised. Until they walked out the locker room door.

The girls had lined up on both sides of the court, making a pathway where Zach waited at the end.

Her heart skipped a beat and she gasped. In his hands were flowers and a microphone. The crowd was silent, and she knew.

Tears flowed from her eyes as Georgia walked her to the man she loved with all her heart.

When they reached Zach, Georgia passed her off to him. He handed the flowers to Emily and took her other hand in his.

"Emily Martin, we have had our ups and downs. And

our misunderstandings. We've played pranks on one another, and yet every time I look at you, my heart whispers *she's the one*. Basketball has brought us together, broken us up, and now I want it to join us together forever."

He knelt on one knee and opened a jewelry box. Astounded, she stared at the diamond ring she had shown him years ago that she liked.

"I bought this ring five years ago with the intention of asking you to marry me. But then I became stupid and made some really bad decisions. I can't promise you that I won't make stupid decisions again, but I can promise you that they will never involve me leaving you.

"For five years, I've grieved losing you, and I don't ever want to be without you again. You told me I was like the Beast and cursed until I found love. I didn't need to find love; it was there in front of me. It's been in my heart since we parted five years ago. Will you marry me, Emily, for better or worse?"

Leaning down, she kissed him on the lips while the gym went crazy. She pulled him to his feet. "Always and forever. I love you, Zach, and nothing would make me happier than being your wife and us living our basketball dreams together."

The band began to play and the crowd erupted with applause and cheers while Emily leaned into Zach and kissed him, her heart filled with love.

When they came apart, the crowd cheered as the two coaches walked to the edge of the court. "Zach, I will never let basketball come between us again, but I have a game to finish. I love you now and forever."

He grinned at her. "Go kick their ass. This game is yours."

She smiled, tears forming in her eyes once again. She gave him a brief kiss and then turned to her team.

"Ladies, thank you for being a part of my engagement. It means so much to me. But now we have to focus. Remember what I told you in the locker room? This game is yours to win. Go out there and make me proud."

The girls leaned in with their hands and they raised them together with a whoop.

The teams took their positions on the court while Emily dried her eyes and watched as her girls fought for the ball.

In the last two minutes of the fourth quarter, the score was tied.

She called a time-out and the girls came over exhausted, huffing and puffing trying to catch their breath.

"You girls are better than them. Don't forget it. Take a deep breath, remember what we've practiced. Remember the video we watched and how they like to drill the ball in the last two minutes. Go, do your best."

The other team looked almost as exhausted as her girls as they met in the middle for the last two minutes.

They raced up and down the court, blocking, setting, and both teams scoring. In the last ten seconds of play, Riley got the ball to Georgia who jumped into the air and let the ball go. Emily held her breath as it hit the rim, bounced into the air, and then sank into the basket.

The buzzer sounded. They had won by two points.

The girls screamed as they ran over to the side of the court and lifted her in the air. It was over. They had beaten the number one team in their division.

Emily looked for Zach who was standing over on the sideline, clapping his hands along with the superintendent and the principal.

She laughed. What a day. What a week. What a life.

# CHAPTER 16

It was her wedding day. Of all places, they had decided to hold it in a place they both loved. In the basketball gym. In the very place they had fallen in love not once, but twice.

A knock on the locker room door let her know it was time.

She wasn't afraid. In fact, this felt perfect.

Her bouquet had flowers coming out of an old basketball with a stem at the bottom for her to hold it. It was perfect.

She opened the door and the principal and the superintendent stood there.

"Are you ready?"

"Yes, and thank you for walking me down the aisle. You two seemed like the perfect choice since my father isn't here."

"We're honored," the principal said.

"Good practice for when Georgia gets married. And no, that's not happening any time soon."

She smiled at them, took their arms and they walked out the door. The girls, her team, were lined up at the center of the court where the Justice of the Peace and Zach waited for her.

Georgia stood up next to her. It seemed only right since the girl was the first one Emily told that she loved Zach. Max stood beside Zach.

A big smile spread across his face.

Basketball season was over. The girls had gone to the UIL tournament but hadn't won the championship, but it was further than Cupid had ever made it, and she felt certain her team would win next year.

Georgia had received a scholarship from Duke, her alma mater. Jayden was going to Texas A&M and Zach was so excited for the kid.

Several other students had received scholarships and their teaching contracts had been renewed.

The last day of school had passed, and she and Zach had the entire summer to honeymoon.

The lawsuit was in the final stages of negotiations, but she didn't care about the money. Her name had been cleared and that was all that mattered.

As a gift to Zach, she wanted to set up a foundation to help abused kids in his brother's name. That was the only plan she had for the money she would receive. But if it helped one child, then it would be worth it.

She stepped in front of Zach.

The Justice of the Peace smiled. "Who gives this woman away?"

The girls on her team, who she loved so very much all screamed. "We do."

The crowd laughed and she took Zach's hand in hers.

Staring into his eyes, she knew that their future would always be filled with games. Lots of games. Loving games.

THANK you for reading Cupid Games, the twelfth book in this series and probably the last. Though I won't rule anything out. I've enjoyed seeing couples find love after making the disastrous choice to dance around the Cupid statue. Zach and Emily were so much fun to write and I hope you enjoyed them as much as I did. Authors love it when readers leave a review, whether it's good or bad.

Hollywood, California

Staring at the envelope in her hand, Jennifer Moss sat in her Volvo waiting to pick up her son from the Hollywood high school baseball practice. Before she left the house, she'd grabbed the mail.

Now, an eerie sense of foreboding spiraled through her and filled her with anxiety. But then every time she received a piece of mail in which she didn't recognize the name on the envelope, her stomach churned.

Could this be from her? How many times had she gotten her hopes up for them only to be dashed? Would this be the same?

A soft breeze blew through the window on the cloudless day. For a moment, she stopped breathing as she stared at the address.

Madison Wilson, Austin, Texas.

Who did she know in Austin? Who was Madison Wilson? Anytime she received an envelope like this, her heart would pound in her chest and she would wonder if she'd been discovered.

Part of her wanted to be found, but then she would think of her life now. No one knew. It had been her secret for twenty-six years.

The memory of the house on Mustang Island overwhelmed her. She'd never returned after that summer, and since her parents' deaths, the house sat vacant. As much as she loved that place, she'd never go back because she would have to face the past.

A past that was heart wrenching and left her scared and hating her family.

Shouts from the field alerted her that the team would be leaving practice shortly. The coach always ended their practice with a pep rally. The kids were a good team and might make it to state this year. For her son's sake, she hoped so.

With a sigh, she tore open the envelope and pulled out the letter.

*My name is Madison Wilson. According to the genealogy report, your DNA and my DNA are linked. It says you're my birth mother. I would like to speak to you and find out why you gave me up for adoption. I would also like to learn my medical background and even see if we have anything in common. If you are willing to speak to me, please contact me at...*

A cry escaped her and the memories flooded her of that

terrible day. Her name was Madison. Her heart leaped with a joy only a mother could feel.

Madison gave her address, her phone number, and even her email address.

It had taken twenty-five years, but her secret was about to be revealed. With a sigh, she stared out at the baseball field and let the memories of that day overwhelm her. How she had clung desperately to her child until her mother ripped the infant from her arms and gave her to the nurse.

She'd never seen the baby again after that day. Tears filled her eyes and trickled down her face. How many times had she thought of finding her and telling her how much she wanted to keep her? In the end, she thought it better not to disrupt her life and had done her best to move on. Now that child was grown up and wondering why she had not been wanted.

But the opposite was true.

Oh, God, how she'd wanted to keep her. To love her and raise her as her own.

That time in her life had been the worst, and she'd never forgiven her mother for forcing her to give up her child for all the right reasons. They were not what Jennifer wanted to hear.

Sometimes doing the right thing was not the easiest. And having that child taken from her arms was gut-wrenching.

Her handsome son walked across the school yard, his head down. Quickly she wiped the tears from her eyes and shoved the letter into her purse.

How was her family going to react to this news?

Her husband Ryan didn't know about her unwed pregnancy and subsequent birth. Her two smart, intelligent, beautiful children had no idea they had a half-sister. This secret had remained hidden for twenty-five years, but no more.

The door opened and her son slid in.

"Hi, Mom," he said and she could see he was upset.

"Bad day?" she asked.

"Kind of," he replied as he looked out the window of the car.

Something had been eating at him and she didn't know what. He refused to talk to her about it, and only said, *I'm okay*. But he wasn't. His grades had gone from honor roll to barely passing and she feared he was going to lose his scholarship to his favorite school.

No matter how she tried to approach him, the walls came slamming down. And today's mail wouldn't make the situation any easier. Yet, she had waited so long for this letter. So long to hear from the baby she loved instantly.

He looked at her and studied her for a moment. "Are you all right?"

"Sure," she said, wondering how he could tell something was up. "Got something in my eye a moment ago."

"Oh," he said and gazed back out the window as she pulled out of the school parking lot.

"Is Dad going to be home tonight?"

"I don't know," she said. "This morning he left early because it's his surgery day."

Alex made a noise she couldn't quite interpret.

Her husband was a leading plastic surgeon in the Hollywood community and had worked on many stars in his practice. The money he brought in had made it easy for her to stay home and raise their two children.

But the hours he worked were sometimes long, and he often came home exhausted. Lately, he seemed to work longer and longer, though he'd promised her he was going to cut back his hours.

In the twenty years they'd been married, she often wondered if she'd traded love for money. Their marriage was good, but they spent so little time together, with him working so many hours. Sometimes it felt like they were two individual people living in the same house.

And there were days she felt lonely. If not for the kids, she would spend her evenings alone. And even they were growing up and moving on with their lives. Taylor would soon finish her second year of college, and next fall, Alex would be going to a university.

"How's the team doing?"

"If we continue to win, we should make the high school playoffs," he said, staring out the window.

Alex was normally so happy and excited and eager to talk, but in the last two months, he'd withdrawn into himself and she couldn't find a way to bring him out. The kid should be so excited about his team making the playoffs, and yet he didn't act like he cared.

Something was eating at her son and she missed the

happy-go-lucky young man who was eager to begin his life.

"That's great news," she said. "When's your next game? Maybe me and your dad can both attend."

Ryan had only made it to one game. One, and soon their son's season and high school career would be at an end. Sometimes she hated Ryan's job, even though their life was luxurious because of his career.

That didn't excite Alex and she knew she had to learn what troubled him.

Sometimes she wished Ryan was an accountant or even a salesman and not a busy doctor.

Maybe after Alex graduated, she would get them reservations at Cozumel and take the kids down to the beach. She doubted that Ryan would take the time off. But it would be good to spend some time with her children.

The thought of Madison crossed her mind and she wondered if she would like to go with them.

"That would be nice," he said. "The next game is Saturday morning."

That was Ryan's tee time. Surely he could give up golfing one Saturday for his son. But nothing came between Ryan and his golf.

They pulled into the drive and the gate opened automatically. She pulled into the back garage. The pool man had been here today, and maybe later tonight, she'd get in the water and swim a few laps.

Closing the garage door, they both exited the car and walked into the house, entering through the laundry room.

"Good afternoon, Mrs. Moss, Alex," the maid said to her. "Dinner is in the oven. I'm leaving for the day."

"Thank you, Esmeralda," she said softly.

Alex walked past the woman and that was so unusual for him. Normally he would hug Esmeralda and tell her the cooking was divine. But not today.

Glancing at her son, Jennifer was worried. Maybe it was time to suggest counseling. Anything to keep his grades from falling even further. Anything to keep him from losing his scholarship. Anything to bring the boy she loved back to her.

"Good night," Esmeralda called as she exited the back door.

Jennifer walked into the massive kitchen and there was a salad sitting out and a casserole ready to turn on in the oven.

"Mom," Alex said, walking back into the kitchen. "Coach said I had to give you this."

She glanced at the envelope he held in his hand.

Taking it, she opened it to the letter inside.

"Damn it, Alex," she said as she read the letter. "What is going on?"

He shrugged. "Don't know."

"If you don't bring your grades up you're going to lose your scholarship. You're about to be kicked off the baseball team. This is not my son. Tell me what's wrong."

With a grimace, he turned and walked out of the kitchen. "Maybe I want to do high school over again. Maybe I'm a loser."

"Alex, don't walk away. Let's sit down and talk about this."

He ignored her and went up the stairs to his room.

Shaking her head, she couldn't wait for Ryan to get home. They had to have a serious talk with Alex, and she had to tell him she had another child. Madison.

Reaching inside the refrigerator, she pulled out a full bottle of wine and poured herself a glass.

It was going to be a hell of a night.

Available at Your Favorite Retailer

**Contemporary Romance**

**Burnett Brides Contemporary Times**

Travis

Tanner

Tucker

Joshua

Jacob

Justin

**Return to Cupid, Texas**

Cupid Stupid

Cupid Scores

Cupid's Dance

Cupid Help Me!

Cupid Cures

**Cupid's Heart

Cupid Santa

**Cupid Second Chance

Cupid Charmer

Cupid Crazy

Cupid's Bachelorette

Cupid Games

Return to Cupid Box Set Books 1-3

Cupid Help Me Box Set Books 4-6

**The Unlucky Bride

**Contemporary Romance**

My Sister's Boyfriend

The Wanted Bride
The Reluctant Santa
The Relationship Coach
Secrets, Lies, & Online Dating

**Bride, Texas Multi-Author Series**
**The Unlucky Bride

**Lipstick and Lead 2.0**
Nailing the Hit Man
Nailing the Billionaire
Nailing the Single Dad

**Secrets of Mustang Island**
Secrets of a Summer Place
Secrets of a Runaway Bride
Secrets From the Past

**The Langley Legacy**
Collin's Challenge

**Short Sexy Reads**
**Racy Reunions Series**
Paying For the Past
Her Christmas Lie
Cupid's Revenge

**Western Historicals**
A Hero's Heart

Second Chance Cowboy
Ethan

**American Brides**
**Katie: Bride of Virginia

**Angel Creek Christmas Brides**
Charity
Ginger
Minnie
Cora

**The Burnett Brides Series**
The Rancher Takes A Bride
The Outlaw Takes A Bride
The Marshal Takes A Bride
The Christmas Bride
Boxed Set

**Lipstick and Lead Series**
Desperate
Deadly
Dangerous
Daring
**Determined
Deceived
Defiant
Devious
Lipstick and Lead Box Set Books 1-4

**** Denotes a sweet book.**

**Want to learn about my new releases before anyone else? Sign up for my New Book Alert and receive a free book.**

USA Today Best-selling author, Sylvia McDaniel obviously has too much time on her hands. With over eighty western historical and contemporary romance novels, she spends most days torturing her characters. Bad boys deserve punishment and even good girls get into trouble. Always looking for the next plot twist, she's known for her sweet, funny, family-oriented romances.

Married to her best friend for over twenty-five years, they recently moved to the state of Colorado where they like to hike, and enjoy the beauty of the forest behind their home with their spoiled dachshunds Zeus and Bailey. (Zeus has his own column in her newsletter.)

Their grown son, still lives in Texas. An avid football watcher, she loves the Broncos and the Cowboys, especially when they're winning.


**www.SylviaMcDaniel.com**

Sylvia@SylviaMcDaniel.com


**The End!**

www.ingramcontent.com/pod-product-compliance
Lightning Source LLC
Chambersburg PA
CBHW061241170626
46809CB00007B/2775